"I expect you to keep the vows you made at our wedding, Laura."

"Vows?" She laughed bitterly, welcoming the pain the memories carried with them, using it to strengthen her courage. "Yes, I made vows to you, Luis, and I meant to keep them. But what about you? How long did you keep your promises? One week, two...possibly three? I would have kept all my marriage vows if you had given me the chance to do so!"

Luis's eyes were black as coal as he glared down at her. "You dare to say that to me after what you did?"

Jennifer Taylor was born in Liverpool, England, and still lives in the northwest, several miles outside of the city. Books have always been a passion of hers, so it seemed natural to choose a library career—a wise decision as the library was where she met her husband, Bill. Twenty years and two children later they are still happily married and she is still working in the library, with the added bonus that she has discovered how challenging and enjoyable writing romance fiction can be!

Books by Jennifer Taylor

HARLEQUIN ROMANCE
3142—LOVESPELL

HARLEQUIN PRESENTS
1326—A MAGICAL TOUCH
1349—TENDER PURSUIT

SPANISH NIGHTS
Jennifer Taylor

Harlequin Books

TORONTO • NEW YORK • LONDON
AMSTERDAM • PARIS • SYDNEY • HAMBURG
STOCKHOLM • ATHENS • TOKYO • MILAN
MADRID • WARSAW • BUDAPEST • AUCKLAND

ISBN 0-373-17248-6

SPANISH NIGHTS

First North American Publication 1995.

Copyright © 1994 by Jennifer Taylor.

CHAPTER ONE

SHE had known that he would find her, known that unbending pride of his would demand he seek her out. All she had hoped to gain by running away was a few months' breathing space, time to gather her strength so that when he did come she would be able to make him listen to her. Now, however, as she saw him standing on the doorstep, his face cold and set, Laura wondered if she was equal to that task yet.

'You'd better come in.' She held the door wide, forcing herself not to flinch as he brushed past her to step inside the narrow hallway. Closing the door, she took a slow breath then turned to face him, letting her eyes linger on the leanly powerful lines of his tall frame, the gleaming blackness of his hair, the smooth pale olive of his skin. He looked little different from when she'd last seen him two months before, his handsome face showing no signs of strain or suffering. Had he missed her, or had he come to find her purely out of a sense of duty? She wished she knew, because maybe then she would know how to handle this meeting.

'You are looking well, Laura. Obviously the English climate agrees with you far more than the Spanish one.' There was faint mockery in his voice and in the dark gaze which traced her soft oval face in its frame of long blonde hair, the huge grey eyes under delicately arched brows, the full curve of her

5

mouth. Laura flushed, self-conscious under the intent scrutiny and achingly aware of the effect those lightly accented tones were having on her. Luis had been educated in England as all his family had, and spoke the language perfectly, but there was always that faint inflection in his deep voice which gave the words a disturbingly foreign flavour. Now Laura let the rich deep tones flow through her, trying desperately to stem the shudder which followed them. She had always found the sound of Luis's voice sensuously stimulating and it seemed that hadn't changed.

'I am very well. However, I doubt you came all this way just to enquire after my health.' She glanced up the stairs, realising that the hall wasn't the best place to hold a conversation, then led the way into the small, old-fashioned sitting-room.

Luis followed her, his eyes skimming the shabby furniture with a hint of distaste which she took immediate exception to.

'I know these aren't the surroundings you are used to, Luis, but if you wish to speak to me then I am afraid that you will have to put up with them. Can I get you anything—coffee, perhaps?'

'No, thank you. I had lunch before I drove down here.' He sat down on one of the over-stuffed chairs, crossing one long leg over the other as he looked up at her with glittering dark eyes. 'Shall we cut out all the pretence of politeness, Laura? It isn't necessary, is it?'

She sat down opposite him, forcing herself to meet his icy gaze. 'No, of course not. So why have you come, Luis?'

He laughed softly, leaning back in the chair so that his head rested comfortably against the cushions as he studied her. 'That is what I like about you, *querida*. You exhibit no shock, ask none of the questions another woman would ask, like how did I find you?'

She arched a brow as she pushed the silky fall of hair back from her face, feeling the tension coiling and uncoiling inside her. Luis might be playing this very low-key at present but she wasn't fool enough to underestimate him in any way. She had hurt him in a way he would never forgive, struck what he saw as a blow against both him and his family, and while she might nurture the hope that the past two months had cooled his anger and made him more responsive to her explanations, she couldn't afford to forget what he had said to her then.

'Why should I ask that? You have the money and the power to accomplish anything you want to, don't you, Luis? It just surprises me somewhat that it has taken you this long to track me down. Surely the name of Rivera isn't losing some of its potency?'

His eyes narrowed, glittering like black ice as they met hers. 'Careful, *querida*. Don't make the mistake of pushing me too far or too hard, will you? Or you might not enjoy the consequences of such an action.'

She laughed bitterly, pain tearing at her heart. 'Could it be any worse than how you treated me a few months ago? Could I be made to feel any lower, any more unworthy of the great honour you bestowed upon me? I am your wife, Luis, yet you treated me like a leper!'

'And is it any wonder? How did you expect me to react, Laura? What did you think I would say when you made your confession?' He leant forwards suddenly, his face set into lines of icily controlled anger as he glared at her. 'Did you really imagine that I would forgive and forget that easily?'

'I thought you loved me! I thought that even though you would be upset, maybe angry at first, that you would listen and try to understand. But you didn't do that, did you, Luis?' She got up and walked to the window, rubbing her hands up and down her arms to ward off the chill that seemed to be seeping deep into her bones. How many times had she imagined this meeting, worked out what she would say, how she would handle it? It didn't matter now because it was all going wrong, all the bitterness reawakening inside both of them. The plain, unpalatable fact was that Luis hadn't loved her enough to accept something that had been a part of her past, and it seemed he still wasn't prepared to do so.

She swung round, her long blonde hair floating around her shoulders as she moved. Impatiently she pushed it back and stared at him, trying to subdue the agony she felt. 'I really can't see that we have anything to discuss, can you? It's obvious that you aren't any more prepared to listen to me now than you were two months ago. I shall be grateful if you would just leave.'

'I'm sure you would but that would be too easy, my sweet wife.' He got up slowly and came towards her, stopping just a few feet away as he subjected her to an insultingly thorough scrutiny. 'You seem to have lost weight, *pequeña*. Have you been pining for me? Maybe it is a good thing that I decided to come now. I had toyed with the idea of leaving our meeting a while longer but...' He shrugged slightly, his shoulders moving briefly under the smooth grey cloth of his expensive suit. As always he was immaculately dressed, the white shirt tailored especially to fit his leanly muscular frame, his handmade leather shoes gleaming despite the fact that it had been raining when he'd arrived. It was part of the image he projected and part of the man, a man who expected perfection in everything he did or touched, even his wife. That had been at the root of the trouble, the reason why their brief marriage had foundered; she hadn't been perfect and Luis hadn't been able to accept that.

She roused herself with an effort, pushing the painful memories to the back of her mind. 'If you are asking if I missed you then the answer is yes. I have missed you, Luis, but not enough to want to go through all the heartache you put me through before. So either tell me what you want or leave. I don't think there is anything left to say, do you?'

'On the contrary, I think we have a lot to talk about.' He reached out to lift a long strand of hair from where it had snagged on her navy sweatshirt, twining it around his fingers in a gleaming, silky chain. 'Do you know that I could have come here weeks ago, Laura, but I didn't. It didn't take me long to discover where you had run to.'

'Then why didn't you come?' She jerked her head, wincing at the painful tug on her roots as the hair remained coiled around Luis's fingers. 'Do you mind?'

'Of course not.' Slowly he uncoiled the strand then smoothed it behind her ear, his fingers brushing lightly against her cheek. Laura shivered then silently berated herself when she saw the knowing glitter in his eyes. Deliberately, she turned her back on him, forcing a cool, impersonal note to her voice to hide her increasing nervousness.

'Look, Luis, if this is some sort of a game then I shall be grateful if you would stop. Rachel will be back soon and I don't want her to be upset by anything she might overhear.'

'I am sure you don't. However, it will be some time before your friend returns. She has an appointment in town, I believe.'

His voice was bland, so why did she feel a sudden flurry of unease, a sense that there was more to that cool statement than there appeared? She swung round to search his face but could find little there to help her. Sunlight was spilling through the window now that the rain had stopped, highlighting the sharp planes and angles of his patrician features, tinting his skin to gold. He was the most handsome man she had ever seen, yet Laura was less aware of that then than she'd ever been as she felt the fear start to run coldly down her spine.

He must have sensed how she was feeling because he smiled with cool arrogance, one dark brow lifting fractionally. 'Aren't you going to ask how I know where Rachel is, *querida*? Or do you imagine that it was a lucky guess?'

His laughter was soft and dark, somehow menacing and Laura felt her heart start to beat faster—too fast. She forced herself to breathe slowly, knowing that she had to hold on to her control until she found out what Luis was planning. 'Nothing you do is luck, Luis. You plan everything, don't you? You don't believe in trusting to luck.'

She was unaware of the bitterness in her tone but he heard it. His face tightened, a nerve beating a furious tempo along his jaw. He took one slow step towards her then stopped so close that she could feel the heat of his body against her breasts.

'And do you blame me, Laura? I trusted you, didn't I? And look how wrong I was to do so.'

She turned her head away, hating to see that icy contempt in his eyes. This man had been her whole world, her moon and stars, everything she'd ever wanted from life, yet it hadn't been enough that she should love him like that. She had made one mistake years ago and he would never forgive her for it.

'I don't see how our quarrel has anything to do with Rachel,' she said quietly. 'She isn't involved in any of this. All she has done is offer me a home since I came back to England.'

'I agree, but sometimes even the most innocent victims find themselves caught up in events. Rachel isn't involved in our "quarrel", Laura, but she will be instrumental in helping us sort out our future life together.'

'I don't know what you mean!' Shock widened her soft grey eyes, stole the colour from her cheeks. 'We don't have a future together, Luis!'

'You are my wife, *querida*. Naturally our two lives will mesh until the day one of us dies.'

His voice was harsh, the accent more pro-nounced now unless it was merely that her senses had been heightened to an unbearable degree. When she made no response he smiled faintly, catching her chin to tilt her face so that he could stare straight into her eyes. 'No protests, Laura? No cries of horror? Maybe this will be easier than I anticipated. Perhaps I should not have wasted so much time these past weeks taking safeguards to ensure your compliance? I should have come to you and told you that I wanted you to come back to me.'

'I...no!' She twisted her head away from his hold, her whole body trembling with shock. 'You don't really want me to be your wife, Luis! You made that more than plain two months ago.'

'We cannot always have the things we want. You *are* my wife, Laura, whether you or I like it or not. And that is the way it shall remain.'

'But why? Are you saying that you love me, Luis? That you want me back because of that?' Hope was like a warm flame in her cold heart, burning brighter and brighter only to be snuffed out when he spoke.

'I am saying that you are my wife and that you shall remain as such. My religion doesn't allow for divorce, if that is what you had been expecting.'

It was hard to stand there while every sweet dream she'd harboured these past lonely months crumbled into dust. It was only pride that stopped her from breaking down, only pride that she had left to see her through. 'What about an annulment? Surely that could be arranged?'

'Perhaps. However, none of my family has suffered the disgrace of such a thing and I have no intention of being the one to cheapen the name of Rivera in the eyes of my countrymen. I expect you to keep the vows you made at our wedding, Laura.'

'Vows?' She laughed bitterly, welcoming the pain the memories carried with them, using it to strengthen her courage. 'Yes, I made vows to you, Luis, and I meant them. But what about you? How long did you keep your promises? One week, two...possibly three? After that they were forgotten. You didn't feel that you had to uphold any promises you had made. *I* would have kept all my marriage vows if *you* had given me the chance to do so!'

His eyes were black as coal from the fires of hell as he glared down at her. 'You dare to say that to me after what you did?'

'I did nothing deliberately! Why won't you accept that?' She was shaking so hard now that she could hardly speak, but she forced the words out.

'Why? That is easily explained. You tricked me, Laura. You deliberately misled me as to your innocence, let me believe that you had slept with no man before you met me so that I would marry you to get you into my bed.'

'No! That isn't true. I didn't try to trick you. I...I just didn't know how to tell you when I was so afraid of what it might do to our relationship. You had built up this picture of me in your mind and I couldn't find the words to tell you the truth, that I had slept with a man before. I loved you so much, Luis. I didn't want to lose you, nor did I want to make the same mistake again by sleeping with you before we married. If I am guilty then it's of once making a mistake I've paid dearly for!'

'A mistake? That's how you see it, is it? And do you see your decision not to tell me the truth as another mistake? Something else you regret but can do little to rectify?' His voice dropped an octave, grating with anger. 'How convenient for you, *mi esposa*, to be able to class all your failings in such gentle terms. You make a *mistake* but it can all be cleared up without too much heartache by means of a simple confession?' He caught her by the shoulders, his fingers biting through the sweat-shirt, bruising her flesh so that she murmured in pain, but he seemed oblivious to the sound as anger claimed him. 'Can you imagine how it felt for me, Laura, to suddenly learn about your mistakes, to discover that my pure and virginal little bride who had determinedly rejected all but the most innocent of advances had slept with another man, maybe other *men*?'

He shook her hard, his eyes pure black with anger now, glittering in a face that seemed set like a mask. 'I have never experienced such anger before, *querida*. I wanted to kill you, do you realise that? I wanted to wring that slender little neck of yours for the way you had deceived me so cleverly. And now you have the audacity to take me to task about not keeping my vows!'

He flung her from him as though he couldn't bear to touch her a moment longer. Laura stumbled back against the wall, leaning against it as she tried to control the pain that was tearing her heart to shreds. 'There weren't other *men*, Luis, just one man! I thought I was in love with him, thought he loved me too, but...' She swallowed down the broken sob, willing him to understand how afraid she'd been both of losing him and of making the same painful mistake again. She had loved him so much but it hadn't blinded her to the differences in their backgrounds. Luis's family had held a position of great standing in his country for centuries, something that his mother had pointed out to her on innumerable occasions. While she had believed that Luis loved her there had always been that fear at the back of her mind that it would all go wrong and she would be left to deal with feelings of both guilt and loss once again.

Now with the knowledge of hindsight she knew that she had been wrong not to tell him about her past before their wedding. It had been love that had made her not do so, and fear, yet he had never been prepared to listen to her pleas.

'Luis, I can't begin to tell you how sorry I...'

He cut her off, his anger under control now. '*Bastante*! Enough. I do not wish to discuss this any further. It will serve no purpose.'

'And I am just expected to accept that, am I? Once again? Well, I'm sorry, Luis, but I *want* to discuss it. I want to talk about it until you finally listen to what I have tried to tell you so many times before!'

'What is there to tell? Do you imagine that I want to hear the intimate details of your affair?' Sarcasm slid like ice through the rich tones, cutting her. It shone in the depths of his eyes as they traced her slim figure, lingering meaningfully on the thrust of her breasts beneath the soft sweatshirt. 'I think I can fill in any gaps, *querida*. It isn't that long since you lay naked in my arms while I made love to you for me to imagine what it was like.'

'That wasn't what I meant! You know it wasn't!' Her face filled with colour as heat flowed along her veins. It was the way he was looking at her as much as what he'd said. She closed her eyes so she wouldn't have to see his expression, but that was a mistake as her mind took full advantage of the moment to unroll a series of shockingly intimate scenes behind her lids: Luis bending to kiss her as his hand slid down her body to caress her breasts; the fire in those devil-dark eyes as he had finally possessed her, his body joining with hers in the ultimate act of love.

Her eyes shot open and looked straight into his for a moment, unguarded, and she felt fire lick along her veins as she saw the echo of all she'd been recalling in those dark depths.

'Luis, I...' She was barely aware of speaking, barely aware of reaching out to him until he turned away with an abruptness that shattered the spell. Her hand fell to her side and she looked down to hide the tears that misted her eyes at the deliberate rejection.

'I will not discuss this further, Laura. It is finished. All there is to discuss now is how long it will take you to pack your things and be ready to leave.'

'Pack? I'm not going anywhere, Luis. Why should I pack?'

'Correction: you are coming with me so you will need your belongings.' He glanced at his watch then back at her, cool and aloof and completely in control as he stood there issuing his orders. But if he thought she was going to meekly fall in line with his wishes then he was sadly mistaken!

'I am not going anywhere with you. Understand?'

'It is you who needs to understand the situation, Laura. You are my wife and as such your place is with me in my home. I have come to take you back with me to Spain. Now you have just over an hour before we need to leave for the airport. Please have your cases ready by then otherwise we shall be forced to leave without them.'

He turned on his heel and strode towards the door but Laura raced after him. She caught his arm, her fingers fastening on the steely hard muscles under the fine cloth. 'Wait a minute! Do you honestly imagine that I am going with you after all you've just said! I may be your wife, Luis, but that doesn't mean you can force me to go anywhere I don't choose to, and I don't choose to go back to Spain!'

He lifted her hand from his arm and carried it to his lips to press a kiss against her knuckles in a gesture which held more mockery than affection. 'I am sure you will change your mind, my sweet. I am sure you will be only too willing to accompany me once Rachel gets back and tells you her news.'

'Rachel? What has this to do with her? I don't understand.' She drew her hand away, rubbing her knuckles down her jeans but it wasn't easy to erase the lingering sensations his kiss had left behind.

'Rachel is crucial to my plan, shall I say? A sort of guarantee that you will do as I wish and resume your place as my wife.' His eyes held hers, something shimmering in their depths, an emotion which made her feel afraid even though she couldn't identify it. 'I could have come to see you many weeks ago, Laura, but the time wasn't right then. I needed to be certain that when we did meet you would find it impossible to refuse my offer. To put it simply, *querida*, if you refuse to come back with me then it won't be you who suffers but Rachel. I know how close you are to her; you've told me many times that she's been like a sister to you, hasn't she, Laura? So will your conscience allow you to see her suffer when you can prevent it? I think not.'

She recoiled from him, closing her eyes as she tried to blank out the sight of that glittering gaze but it was impossible just as it was impossible not to understand what she'd just seen in it. Revenge. That was what Luis wanted now, revenge for the way he thought she had tricked him, revenge for the way that she had run away when she had found it impossible to carry on with their bitter marriage. And in seeking that revenge he would do anything he deemed necessary.

He would ruin her life, and he would ruin Rachel's also without a second thought.

CHAPTER TWO

THE silence was so intense that Laura could hear her own heart beating. There had to be something she could say to make Luis understand how wrong he was to contemplate such a thing, but deep down she knew it would be almost impossible to convince him. Although their marriage had lasted such a short time, she'd fast learned that changing his mind was something Luis rarely did once he'd formed an opinion or decided upon a course of action. How many times had she tried to make him change his mind about *her*? She couldn't even begin to count.

'I see that you are starting to understand now, Laura. Good. I suggest you go and start your packing. We don't want to miss our flight.'

'Understand? I don't understand any of it!' She took a shuddering breath, fighting to remain calm. 'Why should you wish to hurt Rachel? What has she ever done to you?'

'Nothing. I barely know your friend. It is just unfortunate that circumstances dictate I must use her as a means to ensure you do what I require of you.'

'But that isn't fair! Perhaps I can understand you wanting to hit back at me but to hurt Rachel...' she tailed off, searching for the right words to make him understand what a dreadful mistake this was. 'Look, Luis, I can...'

He cut her off abruptly, one long finger pressed to her lips as he stared down into her pale face. 'No, it is you who must look, Laura. You who must understand that you hold the future happiness of your friend in your hands.' He smiled slightly but there was no softening to his expression, no give in his determination to carry through with his plan. 'You do as I ask and Rachel stands to gain from it but if you cross me then you only have yourself to blame for what happens next.'

She turned her head away, shaking all over from a cold that stemmed from fear. 'How? What do you intend to do? For all I know this could be some elaborate bluff to get me on that plane. Why should I go anywhere with you, Luis, when I have no idea what your plan is, or even if you can carry it through!'

His eyes glittered at her undisguised contempt but he spoke quite calmly. Laura would almost have preferred him to shout, to exhibit some signs of anger rather than this icy control that made her realise he must be supremely confident that he could carry out any threats he made.

'Don't doubt that I can do any and everything I threaten, *pequeña*. I never make idle claims. Surely you should know that by now.' He glanced along the hall as a car door slammed outside, mockery lingering like a cold shadow in his eyes as he turned back to her. 'However, it seems that you won't be forced to take my claims on trust, Laura. If I'm not mistaken that is Rachel coming back now. I am sure she will put you completely in the picture.'

He walked away from her without another word, opening the front door and carrying on down the path. He paused briefly to exchange a greeting with Rachel who was just coming in through the gate then climbed into his car and drove away. Laura followed him along the hall, clinging hold of the door as her legs threatened to give way. So much seemed to have happened in such a short time that her head was reeling with it all, but somehow she had to make sense of everything Luis had said and find out what he was up to.

'Are you OK? That was Luis, wasn't it, Laura?' Rachel walked in through the open door, her brown eyes filled with concern as they rested on her friend's pale face. Laura forced a smile, turning away to close the door, using the few seconds it took to get herself under control again.

'Yes. He arrived about half an hour ago. I...I was rather surprised to see him.'

Rachel looked at her uncertainly. 'You were? But you always thought he would come after you, love? You've told me that many times.' She smiled faintly although it did little to ease the lines of strain Laura could see etched on her face. 'I rather think you were hoping that he would come, isn't that right? You still love him, don't you, Laura?'

Laura looked down at the floor, tracing the pattern on the worn carpet with the toe of her shoe. 'I...I don't know what I feel sometimes, Rachel. I'm so mixed up!'

'That makes two of us.' Rachel gave a wry smile when Laura's head came up. 'Sorry, forget I said that. You have enough problems of your own right now. What did Luis want by the way? Did he ask you to go back with him?'

'Something like that. Look, Rachel, what did you mean just now? Has something happened? What was that appointment you had?'

Rachel glanced up the stairs then led the way into the sitting-room and sat down on a chair with a weary sigh. 'I take it that Father has been all right while I've been gone.'

'Fine. I popped up to check on him just before Luis arrived and he was sleeping peacefully. No wonder after the number of times you were up with him through the night. I take it that whatever happened today isn't something you want him to hear about?'

Rachel shook her head, her eyes reflecting her weariness. 'No. I don't want him worrying. He has been through enough lately what with having a second stroke when he was just getting over the first one. This...this is more than he could handle right now.'

To Laura's horror, tears started to run silently down her friend's face, but when she started towards her Rachel waved her away. 'No, please don't. If you give me too much sympathy then I'm afraid that I will fall apart and I can't do that yet. I have to be strong otherwise I won't be able to sort this mess out...*if* I can sort it out, that is.'

Laura sat down on a chair facing her, clasping her hands between her knees to stop them shaking, almost afraid to hear what Rachel had to say. But if something had happened to her friend because of her then she had to know! 'Won't you tell me about it, Rachel? May...maybe I can help in some way.'

Rachel laughed, little amusement in the sound. 'If you have seventy thousand pounds then maybe you can!' She must have seen the shock on Laura's face because she sobered instantly. She ran a weary hand over her face, pushing back the strands of light brown hair. The strain of caring for her father had taken its toll, the sleepless nights leaving shadows under her eyes and etching lines at the corners of her mouth.

Laura had a sudden vivid picture of how Rachel had looked just months before when she, Rachel and Stephanie had set out on that extended holiday together hoping to see something of the world. That was when she had met Luis and fallen in love with him, staying on in Spain to be close to him. Stephanie and Rachel had carried on with the planned itinerary almost to the end, then Rachel's father had suffered a stroke and she'd returned to England to nurse him, while Stephanie had completed the trip and gone to Florida where she'd met and married her husband, Logan. All their lives had been affected by that trip but it wasn't fair that Rachel should suffer now because of her.

'If I had the money I would give it to you, Rachel. You know that. But why do you need it so desperately?'

'Thank you. I know you would. As to why I need such a large sum is simple: to keep a roof over our heads.'

'I don't understand. Are you in some kind of debt?'

'Yes. Remember me telling you that my brother, Jack, had set up a new business venture? Well it appears that Father borrowed the money for it, using this house and some stocks and shares he owns as collateral against the loan. He was confident that between his salary and what Jack would be able to contribute as the business found its feet the loan repayments would be met. Only now this illness of Father's has altered all that. He won't be going back to work and Jack has suffered some sort of setbacks, lost contracts he was banking on. There is no way he can meet even half of the repayments let alone cover the full amount. I...I don't know what's going to happen!'

Rachel ran a hand over her eyes to wipe away the tears. Laura waited silently for her to compose herself, knowing she had to find out if Luis was involved in it all.

'What happened today? Has the bank called in its loan?'

Rachel sighed wearily. 'Father couldn't get the money from the bank. They didn't think it was a good risk to lend it to him. He went to a finance company and they're pressing for their money. Perhaps if Jack hadn't lost those contracts we could have stalled for a bit, offered partial payments or something, but it seems another firm snatched them out from under him.'

'This other firm—do you know the name of it?' Laura held her breath as she felt the links of the chain closing tighter and tighter. She might never be able to prove it but she *knew* Luis was behind it all.

'I can't remember. Something foreign but I was in a bit of a daze by then and couldn't take it all in. All I know is that unless the back-payments are met in full within the next week I shall be receiving formal notification that the loan has been called in.' She gave a stifled sob as the shock and fear resurfaced. 'I don't know which way to turn. Even if I could get a job, which is out of the question with Father so ill, it would take me years to pay this money back and they aren't prepared to wait that long!'

'Surely there must be other contracts your brother can get?'

'He's been trying, believe me. But no matter which way he turns this other company is there before him. It's almost as though they are running some kind of vendetta but that doesn't make any sense because he's never crossed them. The house and everything will have to go and then what will happen to Father? The shock of it all could kill him!'

Laura got up, hugging Rachel as she sobbed out her fears. She felt like sobbing too, only she couldn't afford the luxury of that. Luis was behind it all, of course. He had the money and the power and the ruthless drive. He had known that there was little he could threaten her with on a personal level and cleverly found a far more effective lever in Rachel. Hadn't she herself told him how close the two of them were even though she had never fully explained the reason why? It had been Rachel who had helped her through those dark days at university when her father had died in that terrible accident, Rachel who once again had picked up the pieces when her brief love-affair had gone so disastrously wrong. It had forged a bond of friendship between them that had survived for all these years, so that when Laura had appeared on Rachel's doorstep two months before, Rachel had offered her a place to live and unquestioning support when she had needed it most. Now it was her turn to repay that debt. She wouldn't allow Rachel to suffer in Luis's bid to seek his revenge.

She helped Rachel to her feet and urged her to go upstairs and lie down, hating to see the strain etched on her friend's face. Once Rachel was settled, Laura returned to the sitting-room to wait for Luis coming back. She rested her head against the cushion on the chair and let her mind drift, not trying to block the pictures which filled her mind almost at once. She wanted to remember it all, all the joy and ultimately all the pain and in that way gain strength to do what had to be done.

It seemed like only yesterday, the pictures were so clear and sharp in her head. She had been coming out of a shop clutching a bag filled with bread and cheese for the lunch she was taking back to the small *parador* where she, Rachel and Stephanie had booked a room. They had arrived in Jerez de la Frontera only that morning, intending to stay just the one day, but had discovered that there was so much to see. That afternoon they were going to a display at the Recreo de las Cadenas Palace, headquarters of the famous Andalucian School of Equestrian Art. Laura had been so busy thinking about it that she hadn't noticed the man who stopped to pick up a piece of paper he had dropped.

Cheese and bread had gone flying as Laura had fallen over him, to land stunned on the pavement. Luis had gently picked her up, his deep voice entrancing her as he had murmured apologies. He had insisted on seeing her back to the hotel, charming

her with his impeccable manners, his sophistication, not to mention his stunning good looks.
When he had invited her to dinner by way of an
apology, Laura had eagerly accepted and by the end
of the week, having persuaded the others to stay in
the town, known that she was madly in love with
him.

Even now, after everything that had happened,
she could still recall how it had felt, the excitement,
the aching need to be with him. When Rachel and
Stephanie had decided to continue with their trip,
she had stayed behind in Jerez, finding work in one
of the hotels so that she could be near Luis. He
had asked her to marry him just a few weeks later
and Laura had thought that she had been given
everything she could ever want. She loved him so
much and believed that he loved her. The fact that
he had accepted the limits she placed upon their
lovemaking had highlighted that. Luis had wanted
her, she knew. She could see it in his eyes, feel it
in the leashed tension in his body every time they
kissed but he had respected her desire not to
preempt their wedding night.

Several times Laura had started to tell him about
the brief affair she'd had but always her courage
had deserted her at the last moment. She had loved
him so much; she couldn't bear the thought that
something which had happened so many years
before might spoil what they had. In the end she
had convinced herself that when she did tell Luis
after their wedding he would understand. He might
be angry, even upset, but he loved her and that
would be enough but it wasn't.

Tears stung her eyes as she remembered their wedding-night. The day had been magical, the wedding held in one of the beautiful old churches in Jerez and the reception at Luis's home afterwards like a fairy-tale, and Luis's gentleness and consideration when they had made love later, everything she could have wished for. But afterwards he had been strangely silent, his handsome face set into grim lines. Laura had known then that she had to speak but the words had been strangely difficult to utter in the face of his mounting anger. He had called her names that even now she didn't want to remember, accusing her of lying to him and cheating. He had been more angry than she'd expected yet he wouldn't listen to her halting, desperate attempts to explain and refused to listen as the weeks passed until in the end, Laura couldn't stand it any longer.

She had left, hoping that her leaving might jolt Luis into realising what he was doing to their marriage, but it hadn't done that. He would never forgive her for what he considered to be a deliberate attempt to trick him because the simple fact was that he didn't love her enough.

The sound of a car stopping drew her out of her painful reverie. Laura dried her tears then hurried outside and slid into the passenger seat before Luis could make any attempt to get out and come inside the house. It had been a painful exercise going back over what had happened but it had stiffened her resolve. Her life might be lying in ruins but she wouldn't allow Rachel's world to fall apart as well.

One dark brow was raised mockingly as Luis immediately saw the storm clouds in her grey eyes. 'I see that you and Rachel have spoken?'

Laura ignored the mockery, her voice filled with contempt. 'Yes! I hope you feel proud of yourself, Luis.'

His face tightened, his dark eyes boring into hers. 'I did what was necessary. I took no pleasure from it.'

'I bet you didn't! You are despicable, Luis. Totally and utterly despicable!' She spat the words at him then gasped when he caught her wrist and hauled her to him so fast that she slammed against his body. Anger had set a rim of colour along his cheekbones, thinned his mouth, made his accent even more pronounced when he spoke.

'You forget yourself, *mi esposa*. I will not have you speaking to me like that!'

'Then what do you intend to do about it? Are you going to find some fresh way to punish me for my temerity in speaking the truth? Surely you don't intend to resort to physical violence, Luis? But then there aren't that many options left after what you have already done!'

'Why should you imagine I would have to resort to violence to bring you into line? There are other far more effective ways.' His head came down, his mouth bruising as he kissed her with little regard for her feelings. Laura struggled, beating her fist against his shoulder to make him stop but he merely trapped her hand and twisted it behind her back, drawing her even closer as he forced her mouth open so that he could kiss her with a thoroughness which was an insult by being so devoid of emotion.

When he raised his head to stare arrogantly into her face, she was shaking, silent tears running down her face. He had never kissed her that way before, not even during that bitter lovemaking they had shared. Now she felt cheapened by it, as though he had deliberately set out to teach her how little he cared for her. It was only the thought of what he would do to Rachel that stopped her from leaping from the car and running away again.

'Perhaps you understand now how foolish it is to speak to me in such a way, Laura. I will not tolerate it.'

'I understand perfectly. Don't worry, I won't make the same mistake again. I have no inclination to have you teach me another lesson like that!'

His eyes narrowed dangerously. 'Careful, *querida*. Once again you come within a hair's breadth of going too far.'

'By whose standards? Yours, Luis?' She laughed shrilly, pushing the long blonde hair back from her face. 'That's the real problem, isn't it? I don't meet your exacting standards and you can't accept that. But before we go any further I think we should get a few things straight.'

'You aren't in any position to lay down conditions, Laura. I hold all the cards. Your friend's future lies in my hands. You can merely accede to my wishes and make things easier for her and her family.'

'You would really do this? Cause Rachel and her father to lose their home? You must know that her father is a very sick man and that a shock like this could kill him!'

'But it isn't going to get to that, is it, *querida*? You will ensure that doesn't happen?'

His arrogance fuelled her anger. He knew that she would have to agree to everything he demanded! 'I can't believe that anyone could be this cold-blooded, not even you, Luis, and heaven knows I've had proof of it in the past!'

'I cannot see why you are so surprised. Surely you didn't think I would be prepared to let you go after what you did?'

'It would have been less painful if you had, for you as well as me. Do you really imagine that you will enjoy having me back in the role of your wife knowing that I have been forced into it?'

He shrugged dismissively, running a hand lightly around the steering-wheel. 'You are making this sound far more dramatic than it really is. I just want my wife back, Laura. Divorce is out of the question so it makes sense that we should resume our marriage.'

'And what does your family think of this?' She laughed a touch hysterically. Even for the sake of appearances it was going to be hard to act the part of the loving wife when she knew how Luis felt about her. 'What does your mother feel about having me back as her daughter-in-law? She made it blatantly obvious that she didn't welcome me before and now that this has happened she must feel that all her worst fears about my unsuitability have been confirmed.'

'I have not discussed any of this with my mother or any members of my family. For your information, Laura, everyone believes that you have been away with my blessing.' He smiled at her gasp of surprise. 'You are not the only one adept at keeping a secret, *pequeña*. I kept the reason for your sudden absence a secret also.'

'But how? And why? What did you tell everyone?'

'The how was simple. I merely let it be known that you had returned to England to stay with a sick friend. A small distortion of the truth, you must admit. As for why—well, I didn't see that it would serve any useful purpose to discuss matters that concern no one but us. It is enough that I should have to live with the knowledge of your deceit. To imagine that others were discussing it would be unacceptable.'

He sounded so hard and unyielding that her heart wept. It just emphasised how little his attitude had changed in these past two months. If anything it had hardened because now a desire for revenge had been added to his anger. Had he ever really loved her? Laura doubted it. He had wanted her physically and married her because of that desire, but love? If he had loved her, then surely he would be able to reach beyond his pain and anger?

'I am just surprised that you can bear the thought of having me back, Luis,' she said softly, bitterly. 'Are you sure you can face the thought of sharing your life with a woman like me just for the sake of appearances so that the great name of Rivera won't be damaged in any way?'

'It will not be easy, but there will be compensations.' His voice was equally quiet yet it seemed to strum along her nerves and make her whole body tense.

'What do you mean?'

'I should have thought that was obvious, my love. Our marriage is a fact that cannot be changed so we shall have to make the best of it, enjoy the benefits.' His eyes drifted over her slender body then returned to linger on the bruised swell of her lips in a look she could feel because of its very sensuality. When he suddenly reached over and ran his thumb across her mouth she started violently, her heart hammering until she felt giddy from the fast surge of blood along her veins.

He watched her in silence then slowly withdrew his hand. 'Neither of us can deny that we still find one another attractive. There is still that spark, that hot sexuality, isn't there, Laura? That will be compensation enough . . . for now.'

She reeled back away from him, hating the fact that he understood all the feelings his touch evoked. Their relationship had always been a sensual one even in its darkest moments but she couldn't bear the thought of having him treat her the way he had again. 'I won't let you use me again, Luis.' Her voice was harsh with pain and she saw him frown but she had to make him understand how she felt. 'I couldn't bear to have you . . . touch me the way you did before I left!'

'I don't see that you have any choice in the matter. You are my wife. You will share my life, share my home and share my bed.'

'No!' She reached for the door-handle, desperate to end this painful meeting.

'Yes.' He pulled her back to him, determination etched on his face. 'This will be a marriage in every sense of the word.' He laughed suddenly as he smoothed his hand up her arm and along her shoulder, tracing the delicate bones. 'It won't be such a hardship, Laura, will it? You know that I can make you want me.'

His fingers trailed up her neck to stroke tantalisingly around the curve of her ear, making her shudder in helpless response. He smiled, intent written all over his handsome face as he started to bend towards her, but she pushed him away. 'Stop it!'

'What are you so afraid of, *querida*? You know you want me to kiss you, want to feel my hands on your body.' His hand slid down to her breast, cupping it as he smoothed the nipple with his thumb to bring it surging to life. 'Even though you claim to have hated how I made love to you after I discovered your secret you still responded to me as you are responding to me now.'

His words filled her with shame and she closed her eyes against the truth of what he said. She had both hated and longed for his touch. He had been able to rouse her to mindless passion, making her cling to him and call out his name, yet there had been no love in his lovemaking, just a cold, clinical desire to impose his will on her as a punishment. Now the thought of having him treat her that way again was too much.

Tears ran unheeded down her cheeks as she waited to feel his mouth claiming hers in a kiss that would reflect all her fears, so that it took a moment to realise that he was drawing away from her. She opened her eyes, trying to understand why he had changed his mind, but there was little to be gleaned from his expression. He obviously understood her confusion because he smiled coldly as he gestured towards the road.

'This is neither the time nor the place. I prefer to kiss you somewhere more private where we won't be interrupted.'

Her heart sank, the hope that had started to blossom wilting. She was a fool to imagine that he might care about her feelings! 'I hate you, Luis!'

'Do you?' He shrugged dismissively. 'I'm afraid it's of little consequence now. Have you done as I asked and packed your things ready to leave?'

'No! How can I go when Rachel is so upset because of what you've orchestrated?'

'And how can you stay when doing so jeopardises her future even more? Don't play games with me, Laura. You will not win, be sure of that.'

'I am not playing games! Even you must see that I can't walk out on her today now that this has happened.' Icy contempt laced her angry voice but he was unperturbed by it.

'Rachel is an adult. She doesn't need you to hold her hand.'

'No, she doesn't, but she does need support, something to get her through this mess.' She stopped, struck by a sudden thought. 'You do intend to sort this out? You aren't just trying to trick me, making me believe that it will all be cleared up if I go with you only to find that you have done nothing to solve Rachel's problems?'

'I shall start the process as long as I have your word that you will accompany me back to Spain tonight.' He paused to study her with cool hauteur. 'However, Laura, I am not a fool, so do not make the mistake of taking me for one, will you?'

'I don't know what you mean.'

'No? Perhaps I am being overly cautious but I prefer to foresee all eventualities. That being the case, I shall, as I said, start the process to ease Rachel's financial problems by ensuring that her brother gets this new contract he is bidding for. It will enable him to pay something towards the loan, enough to satisfy the finance company at least. However you must always remember that your friend's future security depends upon your own behaviour.' He smiled briefly at her shocked expression. 'You behave as the wife of Luis de Rivera should and there will be no problems for her. But if you do anything foolish, Laura, like running away again, then Rachel will bear the consequences. You have just this one chance to save your friend. Is that clear?'

'Oh, I understand. All of it! You are despicable, Luis. Totally and utterly despicable. Have you no heart at all?'

Anger shimmered in his black eyes, burning her with its heat as he bent towards her. 'No. If I ever did have a heart then you destroyed it, Laura. You, with your lies and deceit!' He drew back abruptly, glancing at the thin gold watch strapped to his wrist. 'There is a flight at seven this evening. I shall re-book our seats for then. Make sure that you are ready when I come for you, *querida*. I shall accept no excuses and make no allowances. Your future and that of Rachel and her family lies in your hands.'

He started the engine, waiting while she got out before driving away. Laura watched him go with a pain so great tearing at her heart that she felt as though it was being ripped to shreds. There was no way she seemed able to break through that wall of ice he'd surrounded himself with. He hated her for what he saw as her deliberate treachery, and she hated him for the way he was prepared to do anything to make her pay.

How could they make a life together founded on such bitterness and hatred? They would end up by destroying each other, yet there seemed no way out, when Luis was so determined to get his revenge.

CHAPTER THREE

LAURA settled back as the plane started its descent. Their flight had been delayed so that by the time they had changed planes in Madrid to fly on to Jerez de la Frontera, where Luis lived, they had been travelling for several hours. Now she could feel weariness enveloping her but she couldn't afford to relax. There was still the coming meeting with Luis's family to get through.

She glanced round at him and felt a sudden stab of fear. How could they hope to convince everyone that theirs was a proper marriage when they felt the way they did?

He must have felt her gaze because he looked up suddenly, his expression shuttered. What was he thinking, feeling? Was he worried about this coming meeting as she was, or was that cool confidence of his so great that he was certain it would all go as he had planned?

'What is it, Laura?' His voice was quiet so that it wouldn't carry to the seats behind, but she started nervously. 'If there is a problem then I wish to hear about it before we reach the house, so what is worrying you now?'

She laughed bitterly. 'Arriving at the house is what's worrying me, Luis! There's no way that people are going to believe this marriage of ours is a love match!'

Her voice had risen to carry clearly to the elderly couple seated behind them and Luis's face tightened as his fingers fastened around hers on the arm of the chair. 'That is enough. No one will believe it if you act like that! Remember that it is up to you what happens to your friend. You must convince my family that our marriage was founded in heaven and that we couldn't be happier.'

The cold, hard sarcasm hurt and Laura looked away as her eyes misted with tears. How could he hope to fool his family and friends when every word he said betrayed his hatred of her? 'It won't work, Luis. Nobody is going to believe that we are madly in love.'

'No?' He reached over and turned her face to his. 'People will see what we want them to see and believe what we want them to believe. It's as simple as that.' His voice dropped an octave, dark and deep and deliciously sensuous as he bent closer to her. 'We still feel passion for one another, that same desire that brought us together once before. Others will see that and misinterpret it as love.' He ran his thumb across her mouth and smiled at her soft indrawn gasp of breath. 'Heaven knows I was fool enough to make that same mistake myself, so there is no reason why others won't make the same one as long as you play your part as well as I know you are capable of. You are an accomplished actress, *mi esposa*, so now it is up to you to put your talent to full use again.'

She snatched her head away. 'I keep telling you, Luis, that it wasn't an act! I loved you. I wanted to marry you but I never set out to trick you.'

'And that was why you lied to me? You made me out to be a fool, Laura, and if that is your idea of love then I am only glad neither of us feels that way any longer.'

He turned away, his face stern and remote once more. Laura swallowed down her pain. He would never understand; she had struck a blow against that fierce pride of his and he would never forgive her for that. It would always lie between them, and not for the first time she wished she could turn back the clock and erase that brief love-affair she'd had while she was at university. But that was impossible. It was a part of her past that had formed her into the woman she was today, and if Luis couldn't accept that then he could never accept her.

It was almost dark when the chauffeur-driven car turned into the drive of the Casa de Flores, Luis's home. Conversation had been non-existent on the short drive from the airport. Luis had seemed engrossed in his own thoughts and Laura had shied away from making conversation when all it seemed to do was lead to arguments.

Now she sat silently as the car made its way up the sweeping driveway. It was so dark that she could barely see the rolling acres of vineyards where the Palomino grapes were grown. Luis's family owned a small *bodega* by comparison to some in the area but the sherry they produced was the finest quality and much sought after throughout the world. In recent years demand for sherry had decreased as the drink had become less fashionable, so that thousands of acres were being uprooted to prevent a glut on the market which would bring prices down. But the wine the Riveras produced was still in great demand, especially in Holland where fine dry sherries were still so popular. By any standards Luis was a wealthy man who held a position of power and standing in the community, and she would be expected to live up to those exacting standards. It was a thought which filled her with fear in the present circumstances.

'There is no going back, Laura. You gave me your word and you must understand the consequences of going back on it.'

How had he known what she was feeling? She had no idea but it shook her. In silence she watched as the house came closer, feeling tension coiling in her stomach. Luis's family had never really welcomed her, making it plain that they would have preferred him to marry someone far more suitable to their lifestyle but he had been determined. How he must be regretting it now!

Her eyes were haunted as she climbed out of the car but Luis appeared not to notice as he dismissed the chauffeur and took her arm to escort her up the steps and in through the huge double oak doors which led into an enormous black- and white-tiled entrance hall. An ornate brass and crystal chandelier reflected off the heavy dark oak furniture, highlighting the patina of centuries. Luis's family had built the house in the seventeenth century and lived there ever since, a fact that Doña Elena had never tired of reminding Laura about to emphasise the differences in their backgrounds. Now, as she heard the click of heels on the tiled floor behind them, she steeled herself for the coming meeting.

She turned slowly then felt herself go cold when she saw the woman standing there, a woman she had learned to mistrust even more than Luis's mother.

'You are late, Luis. Doña Elena sends her apologies but she has retired for the night. I offered to stay to meet you instead.' Mercedes Lorca came forwards, her dark eyes flickering from Luis to Laura as she moved with her customary sinuous grace. As always she was immaculately dressed, her black hair smoothed into a classical chignon, her full lips tinted red to match the slim-fitting dress which hugged her voluptuous figure. Laura was instantly conscious of her own travel-weary state and knew without a doubt that had been Mercedes's intention.

She stiffened under the cold scrutiny, seeing beneath the veneer of politeness. Mercedes had hated Laura from the outset, barely hiding her animosity whenever they were alone. From what Laura had gleaned, everyone had expected Luis to marry *her*, a marriage which would have been a suitable bonding of two people from similar backgrounds and the joining of two important sherry producing families.

Laura could have accepted and made allowances for Mercedes's hostility in those circumstances and even have attempted to win the other woman over. What she couldn't accept was the way the older woman had deliberately set out to drive a wedge between her and Luis. After Luis had found out about her past, it had been Mercedes he had turned to for comfort, and that was something Laura could never forgive or forget!

'Laura, how are you? I don't know if your stay away from us has done you any good. You look extremely tired.'

The smile on the older woman's face might have fooled some, but it didn't fool Laura. She stared coolly back, keeping the anger from her voice so that Mercedes wouldn't know she had scored a point. 'It has been a tiring journey and a tiring few months. It is probably a good job that Luis insisted I return now. Being here with him will soon cure my tiredness.'

She slid her hand into Luis's arm, watching the quick flash of anger in Mercedes's eyes before she carefully concealed it. With a non-committal murmur the woman led the way towards the small salon, leaving Laura and Luis to follow.

'And what was that all about? I will not tolerate you being rude to guests, Laura.' Luis's voice was steely as he drew her back but all of a sudden she didn't care. How many times had she suffered some spiteful comment Mercedes had made rather than cause a scene.

'I was as polite as Mercedes was. You might not be able to see what she is up to but I am not blind to her tricks.'

'And what tricks are those?' He moved closer, smiling faintly when she started nervously as his arm brushed the side of her breast.

'She...she has never liked me. She has done everything in her power to put a wedge between us and ruin our marriage.'

He laughed harshly. '*She* has done that? If anyone has ruined our marriage it is you, *querida*.'

'Maybe I am to blame, but if Mercedes hadn't welcomed you then maybe we could have talked things through. If she hadn't been so quick to offer comfort, Luis, we might have had a chance to resolve our problems.'

'You really think it could have been that simple? If Mercedes had closed the door on our friendship then we would still be enjoying a real marriage, not this mockery?' His anger was rising but hers spiralled to meet it as she remembered the pain and heartache she'd felt on realising that Luis had turned to another woman for comfort.

'Closing the door to you wasn't the only thing she should have done. She should have kept you out of her bed as well, Luis!'

He went still, his body rigid then suddenly he laughed in a way which sent a disturbing shudder through her. He cupped her cheek with one hand, his fingers smoothing its softness to leave behind a trail of fire and a turbulence of emotions which deafened her to what he was saying. It was only when she noticed the cold mockery on his face that she dragged herself free of the sensuous spell.

'What...what did you say?' Her voice was husky, betraying, and she saw his smile deepen.

'I said that it was flattering to realise that you could still be jealous about me and other women, Laura. Especially in view of the fact that you have been at great pains to tell me how you no longer feel anything for me.'

'I am not jealous. I'm not! I don't care who you see or who...'

'I sleep with? Is that what you are trying to say, *pequeña*? How understanding of you. A man is lucky to have a wife like you, a woman who understands his peccadilloes.'

Laura turned her head away, afraid of what he might see in her expression. She shouldn't feel jealous of Luis and Mercedes or of him sleeping with any other woman. She hated him! It didn't matter whom he took to his bed and made love to! Yet the thought of him holding another woman in his arms and murmuring to her as his hands stroked her flesh as he had once done with her was almost more than she could bear.

In silence she let Luis lead her to the small, elegant salon where Mercedes was pouring coffee from a heavy silver pot into wafer-thin cups. She glanced up as they walked into the room then smiled with a faint satisfaction when she saw the tension that was evident between them. Handing them both cups of the fragrant brew, she sat down on one of the silk-covered chairs and spoke to Luis in rapid Spanish before breaking off with a false little laugh.

'Oh, forgive me, Laura. I keep forgetting that your knowledge of our language is limited. You really must make an effort to learn it properly now that you are back again. That is, assuming that you intend to stay this time.'

The woman's voice was bland but Laura shot a quick look at Luis. He had said that he'd told no one about what had happened but did that include Mercedes? Suddenly she couldn't stand the thought of the woman knowing her secret and gloating about what it had done to her marriage. However before she could say anything Luis took her hand and raised it to his lips.

'Laura has promised me that she will be staying here with me from now on. Isn't that so, *mi esposa*?'

His words were a parody of the truth. Laura glared at him, taking care that Mercedes didn't see the look she gave him. 'Yes. You know I did, darling.'

Mercedes obviously didn't like the exchange, missing the undercurrents. She set her cup down then stood up and smoothed her dress over her hips. 'I am sure that your mother will be pleased to hear that news, Luis. Laura's prolonged absence has caused her some concern and in her state of health that is something I am sure you wish to avoid.'

'Of course. I am grateful for the time you have devoted to her recently, Mercedes. With my sister away studying in Paris and I going to England to collect Laura, Madre would have been on her own these past few days.'

Mercedes smiled with satisfaction, shooting a look at Laura who was silently watching the exchange. 'What else should close family friends do, Luis? You know that I am only too pleased to help in any way I can.' She gave a tinkly little laugh which grated on every one of Laura's overstretched nerves. 'After all, I have been such a frequent visitor to this house over the years when we were growing up that it is almost my second home! Now if you will both excuse me I must go.'

'How did you get here? By car? I didn't notice it outside.' Luis stood up, his smile warm and natural. They made such a perfect couple, Laura thought with a pang of regret, both tall and elegant and aristocratic. Did Luis regret not marrying

Mercedes instead of her? Maybe if she had listened to the advice people had tried to give her before they married then they wouldn't all be in this mess now. But she had loved Luis so much that it had closed her mind to reason. And now she would have to pay the price.

'My car is in the garage for repair. Some tiresome problem with the gearbox, I believe. Domingo drove me over this afternoon. I shall ring home and see if he can collect me.'

'There is no need to do that, Mercedes. Naturally I shall be only too pleased to drive you home.' Luis laughed. 'Anyway, knowing that brother of yours, I doubt he will be in at this time of the night!'

'If you are sure it isn't too much trouble.' Mercedes turned to Laura, not bothering to hide her triumph. 'I hope you don't mind, Laura.'

'Of course not.' Laura determinedly held her own smile, refusing to let the other woman know how much she disliked the idea. She got up and walked into the hall with them, forcing herself not to flinch when Luis bent and pressed a cool kiss to her cheek.

'I won't be long,' he said politely. 'You must be tired after your journey though so don't wait up for me.'

Her eyes glittered back into his, letting him know exactly what she thought of his advice and the reasons for it. 'Don't worry, I shan't. Take your time, darling. There's no need to rush back on my account. I'm sure that you and Mercedes must have a lot to catch up on.'

His mouth thinned at the barely veiled sarcasm in her soft voice, his expression promising retribution when he returned, but rashly Laura didn't care. She was tired of bowing to his whims and following his orders. It was about time she showed him he might come to regret forcing her to return like this.

However, her bravado lasted little longer than it took for Luis to escort Mercedes to the car. Was this going to be the pattern for many nights to come? Would she be left alone here while Luis spent his time with other women? If that was so then she didn't know how she was going to bear it. Luis had set out to seek revenge and from the look of it he was going to be successful, because there wasn't a thing she could do to stop him.

Laura didn't expect to sleep but exhaustion had taken its toll. She fell into a restless sleep, to awaken several hours later with panic clawing at the edges of her consciousness. She sat up in the huge bed and took gulping breaths of air while she fought against the nightmares, but it took a long time for them to go.

Being back in the house and in this room she and Luis had shared had served to heighten the dreams which had haunted her for months. Now it seemed impossible to clear the images from her mind and she moaned softly in distress.

'What is it, Laura? Are you ill?' Luis's voice was soft but she gave a sharp cry of alarm. He muttered something rough half under his breath and came further into the room, leaving the door from the dressing-room wide open so that light spilled into the bedroom. Laura shrank back from the glare, turning her face away as Luis stopped beside the bed.

'I asked you a question, Laura. What is wrong?'
He sounded more angry than concerned and Laura
reacted instantly to it. She glared back at him, her
face paper-white in the cold light, her eyes shadowed with remnants of the dreams.

'Nothing! I am fine. You don't need to worry
about me, Luis. I mean, what could possibly be
wrong when I have just returned to my husband's
loving care?'

'Enough! Why do you keep trying to goad me
like this? What purpose does it serve?' He sat down
on the side of the bed. He was still wearing the
elegant suit trousers and white shirt he'd worn
earlier, although he had shed his jacket and removed his tie, unbuttoning the front of the shirt so
that she could see his tanned, hair-roughened chest
through the opening, and despite herself Laura felt
a ripple of hot awareness run through. Deliberately
she moved her gaze away, whipping up her anger,
afraid of the feelings she could feel stirring to life.

'Purpose? It just reminds me what a bastard you
really are, Luis!'

His eyes darkened but surprisingly there was a
trace of amusement in his deep voice rather than
the anger she'd expected. 'And do you *need* to
remind yourself of that fact, *querida*? Is it easy to
forget that you hate me?'

Too late she realised her error. She edged away
from him, feeling the coolness of the fine percale
sheets against her thighs where the gown had ridden
up. 'No, it isn't easy to forget what you are. I don't
think I shall ever be able to do that.' She laughed
bitterly, pain and anger surfacing in almost equal
measures as she swept a glance at the bedside clock.

'I hope you didn't outstay your welcome at Mercedes's home. But of course I tend to forget that you and she are such old *friends*. I am sure that she enjoyed entertaining you until the early hours.'

His laugh sent a shiver down her spine. He bent towards her to tilt her chin while he studied her face. 'Do I detect more than a hint of jealousy, my devoted little wife? Tut, tut, you know that I only have eyes for you.' He bent towards her but Laura quickly turned her head away before he could kiss her on the mouth. She pushed against his chest, feeling the warmth of his body on her palms as she tried to move him away from her.

'No! Do you imagine that I would welcome you when you've been with her? I might be forced to continue with this marriage to save Rachel but there is no way I shall put up with this, Luis!'

'And what if I tell you that I spent only ten minutes at Mercedes's home talking business with her father? Would that make a difference to the welcome I would get from you?'

'I wouldn't believe you. You must think me a fool, Luis. I know what time you left here to drive her home!'

'But you don't know what time I arrived back because you were already fast asleep, worn out by all the trauma, I imagine.' He moved closer, effectively trapping her against the carved headboard. 'You cannot imagine how charming you look fast asleep, Laura, wearing that very fetching gown.' His eyes skimmed the thin white silk nightgown before returning to her face. 'I was tempted to wake you but, being a considerate husband, decided to let you rest undisturbed and spend the night in my dressing-room. However, that doesn't seem necessary now, does it, *querida*?'

His hand slid softly up her arm, his fingers brushing so lightly against her skin that she could feel every tiny nerve-ending tingling with sensation. Desperately she pushed his hand away, all too aware of the throbbing ache that was springing to treacherous life inside her. She wouldn't let Luis use her this way!

'Stop that!'

'Stop what? This?' Once again his hand made a slow, maddening foray over her bare skin, lingering on the point of her shoulder before moving to the delicate bones of her throat while he caressed the long smooth lines of it with his thumb. Laura shuddered, her hand catching his to move it away but instead of gaining the advantage she lost it when Luis turned his hand over and captured hers, holding it while he pressed his mouth to the spot where his fingers had been.

'No... please, Luis.' Her voice was weak when she wanted it to be strong. It held a hoarse note which betrayed her real feelings and against her throat she felt him smile. Slowly, deliberately, he ran his mouth over her skin, the tip of his tongue tracing a delicate pattern on the soft white flesh. Laura murmured something unintelligible, feeling flames of desire licking along her veins. She didn't want to feel this way, didn't want her body to respond to his touch, yet she seemed powerless to resist now as she had been powerless to resist all those weeks before. Could she bear to go through all that pain, to have Luis make love to her when what he felt was so alien to love?

'Don't do this, Luis, please. It won't help either of us. You know it won't.' Her eyes were dark with memories when they met his but it did little to stop him.

'I disagree. This will do a lot to help me, Laura. I have dreamt of this night after night. Dreamt of having you back here in my bed and making love to you. Yes, this will go a long way to help me feel whole again, *mi esposa*!'

His head came down so suddenly that she had no chance to avoid the kiss. His lips took hers with a brutal force and scant regard for her feelings. If he had intended to hurt her and pay her back then he couldn't have found a more bitterly effective way as he plundered her mouth. When he finally drew back she was shaking all over, her eyes glazed with tears.

'I know you hate me, Luis, but this is cruel!'

'Hate you?' He drew back further to study her face, his eyes filled with an emotion she found it hard to define. 'Yes, I have hated you these past weeks, hated and detested everything you have done to me, to our marriage, yet, strangely, hatred isn't the strongest emotion I am feeling right now.' He reached out and caught her around the waist, lifting her to him so that her body lay against his, letting her feel the urgency of his arousal. Her eyes lifted to his, wide and shocked, and she saw him smile with a wry, almost bitter self-mockery.

'Yes, I want you. You can tell that, can't you, Laura? I want to make love to you, bury myself in your sweet softness, stroke that smooth satin skin,

pretend just for a while that you are what I believed
you to be when I married you.'

'No! You can't pretend like that, Luis! You can't
pretend that nothing has changed when you know
that it has. You either accept my past or...'

He cut her off abruptly, his hands tightening so
that she murmured a protest but he seemed not to
hear. 'I shall never accept it, Laura. Never!'

'Then there is no point in this...in any of it.'
She twisted in his hold but he held her firmly,
drawing her closer so that she could feel every rigid
inch of his body imprinted against her softness.

'But I disagree, my sweet. I find the idea of
making love to you too tempting to resist, so why
try? We are married and it is my right to do so.'

Her eyes blazed back at him. 'Right? There are
no such things as "rights" in this situation. You
intend to use force to make me bow to what you
want, and there is a name for that, Luis: rape!'

'Such an ugly word to come from such a beautiful
mouth.' He ran a fingertip around her mouth,
holding her as she struggled. 'I have no intention
of using force, though, *querida*. You hurt me by
making such an accusation.' He laughed softly as
he moved his fingers once again across her lips then
trailed them lightly along her jaw. 'Force won't be
necessary because you will want me to love you so
much that you will beg for my touch, plead with
me for the release that only I can give you.'

'You really are the most insufferably egotistic...'

The rest of the heated words were lost as he bent
and kissed her, his lips surprisingly gentle now.
Laura tried to draw away, recognising immediately
the danger of the kiss, but he merely weaved his

fingers through her hair and held her head still while he traced her lips with the tip of his tongue, inviting them to part for him. Laura clamped her mouth tightly shut. She would never give in, would never do as he had said and beg!

'But why are you being difficult? You know you enjoy my kisses as much as I enjoy giving them to you.' His voice was deep velvet, his accent strumming lightly through the words and making her tingle with awareness and need. She shook her head, wanting him to understand that she wouldn't do what he wanted willingly before her strength gave out and she capitulated.

'No, Luis! You're wrong. I don't want your kisses or anything at all from you.' There was desperation in the denial and she saw him smile before he bent to brush his mouth along her jaw in a trail of soft, fleeting kisses that left behind them trickles of fire.

'Perhaps your mind is telling you that you don't want me—but your body, Laura. What is that telling you?' His hand slid down her throat, his fingers brushing across the swell of her breasts, bare above the deep neckline of the nightgown. Back and forth they stroked, so gently yet so devastatingly that she felt the sensations to the tips of her toes. When his fingers swept lower, she gave a sharp cry of protest and caught his hand to move it away from her body.

'Please, Luis! This isn't right. It isn't even sensible! You must know that?'

He shrugged as he lifted her hand to his lips to kiss her fingers. 'Perhaps, but I am not listening to my head now, *pequeña*. I am listening to what my

body is telling me of its wants, its needs, and I want
you whether it is right or sensible.'

Slowly he set her hand down on the covers then
cupped her breast, his thumb teasing the already
rigid nipple until she gasped half in protest, half in
pleasure. 'See, Laura, I am telling the truth, am I
not? You do want me. You want me no matter that
your head tells you otherwise!'

He took her mouth in a searing kiss, pinning her
against the pillows as his hands swept down the
curves of her body, stroking the smooth silky skin
until every inch of her felt as though it was on fire,
burning with desire for him. Laura murmured a
protest, her hands pushing at his broad chest, a
shudder running through her when her fingers en-
countered hard muscle and warm flesh. And what
had started as an attempt to make him stop ended
abruptly.

Just the feel of him under her hands, the heat of
his skin, the pounding beat of his heart against her
palm, made her feel dizzy. Hands that had meant
to repulse him started to caress, smoothing over the
hair-roughened skin, feeling the softly abrasive
sensation making her palms tingle as unconsciously her actions mirrored his. He groaned softly
in his throat, his body tensing under the light touch
of her hands and a sudden surge of intense satisfaction shot through her that she could make him
feel this way despite everything that had happened.
Was it possible that he felt more for her than he
admitted to feeling and that this act of love could
unlock the door to those feelings?

Just the thought drove any lingering ideas of resisting from her head as she drew him closer and

opened her mouth to kiss him back just as passion-
ately as he kissed her. When his hands slid almost
roughly to the thin straps of her gown and pulled
them down to bare her breasts so that he could tease
the hard nipples with his teeth and tongue, she
helped him, moaning at the hot spirals of sensation
that filled her. She had dreamed of Luis's touch for
so long and now it seemed all those dreams had
come true.

He stripped her quickly, his hands returning to
her body almost before she had chance to miss them
as he stroked her hips, her thighs, the calf of each
leg, the arching instep of her slender feet. Laura
felt boneless, her body responding helplessly to each
caress with an ever increasing desire that had her
writhing against the sheets. When Luis broke away
to drag his own clothes off she watched him with
passion-drugged eyes, her arms opening to enfold
him as he came back to her.

'Do you want me, *querida*?' His voice was husky
and warm, the liquid tones dark with promise and
she smiled against his mouth as she pressed kisses
to the thinly sculpted lips.

'Yes. You know I do, Luis.'

'Then tell me, Laura. Tell me how much you want
me.' He brushed her breast with his mouth then let
his lips travel up her throat, nibbling at the pulse
that was beating there so rapidly. Laura smiled,
arching towards him, feeling her breasts brushing
against his chest, her thighs tangling with his, the
hardness of his body which betrayed his own desperate needs.

'I want you more than anything, Luis. I want
you to make love to me...now!' Her own voice

was husky and betraying. There was no reason to lie, no reason to pretend when Luis felt the same as she.

When he suddenly moved over her, she closed her eyes, feeling the magic possessing her as his body slid into the most intimate contact of all with hers and started to drive them both to dizzying heights. Laura moaned her need, biting his shoulder to stem the frenzied cries.

'You want me, Laura, don't you?' There was a harsh triumph in his voice now, an echo of something that brought her eyes open, and she stared into his face with shock, seeing the anger that lay in the depths of his black eyes as he drove them both towards the brink of fulfilment.

'No...no. No, Luis!' The denial whispered from her lips as her body betrayed her, spinning towards fulfilment, tricked into a completion that had been born out of hatred and nothing else. When Luis got up and left her without a word, Laura rolled into a tight little ball, unable to cry out the hurt and pain as night faded and brought with it a new day, and the promise of so many days to come. And in all those days and all those nights there would be no love, just this cold, bitter hatred. How could she bear it?

CHAPTER FOUR

SUNLIGHT slanted through the window, gilding the white sheets and antique lace spread which lay in a tumbled heap on the bed. Laura averted her gaze, hugging her arms around herself, but despite the warmth of the morning sun she felt cold, chilled to the bone by what had happened.

What a fool she had been to let Luis trick her that way, to allow emotion to cloud reason. He had made it plain from the outset what he intended yet she, like a fool, hadn't really believed him. Now she had no reason to doubt that he was out for revenge and no reason to hope that his attitude towards her would ever soften.

The dressing-room door opened suddenly and she started nervously but it was only Pilar, the young housemaid. Laura forced a smile for the girl's shy apology for the intrusion, only too aware of the speculation in Pilar's dark eyes. There was bound to be talk about her and Luis now that she had come back and she would have to learn to live with it. But that didn't mean it was going to be pleasant always knowing that she was the subject of gossip.

There was a light of battle in her eyes as she left the room and went downstairs and out to the terrace but it did little to quell the sudden wild flurry she felt when she found Luis seated at the white, wrought-iron table. It was obvious that he had been up for some time because he was dressed in an open-necked white shirt and creamy-white breeches tucked into soft black leather boots. Most mornings he made time to ride one of the horses he kept at the stables behind the house and it seemed that this morning was no exception.

He glanced up as she came on to the terrace then stood up and held the chair for her with his usual impeccable show of manners. Once she was seated he poured her coffee from the ornate pot and handed it to her as though it was a routine they had followed forever. Laura took a sip of the strongly fragrant brew, striving to stay calm, but when she suddenly looked up and saw the mockery in his eyes she lost the battle.

'I imagine you are feeling very satisfied with yourself, aren't you, Luis? You taught me lesson number one last night.'

He toyed with his cup but stared calmly back at her. 'I had no intention of teaching you anything you didn't already know, Laura. You want me, I want you. Simple facts, don't you agree?'

'No, I don't! I don't agree with any of this…this charade! But don't try it again. Do you hear me? because if you *ever* do what you did last night then I…'

'You will…what?' He leant forward so suddenly that she couldn't avoid him as he pulled her to him, so close that she could smell the musky scent of the sandalwood soap he always used, the richness of leather from when he'd been riding. The scents stirred her senses, threatening to cloud her mind, but she fought the weakness by remembering how he had humiliated her.

'I shall find something. Some way to make you sorry you ever started this!'

He laughed softly as his fingers slid from her wrist to her elbow in a light caress. 'I am quaking in my shoes, isn't that the expression you use, *querida*? The thought of what you might do to punish me . . . !' He laughed again, arrogance in the tilt of his head, the curve of his mobile mouth, and Laura felt her temper flare out of control. Without a thought to the consequences she struck out at him, but he was far too quick for her. His hand shot out and captured hers, his fingers biting into her flesh as his eyes blazed back at her for a long moment before he brought himself under control again. Turning her hand palm upwards, he pressed a kiss to its centre then closed her fingers over the warm spot where his lips had touched.

'I hate you, Luis!' she spat back at him, struggling to free herself.

'So you have said repeatedly over the past couple of days. Do you think I care how you feel, Laura? Do you think it will influence me in any way?' He let her go to pick up his cup and take a drink of the coffee before putting the cup down again with a hand that was rock steady. 'It doesn't bother me how you feel or what you think. You lost any right you had to expect consideration from me when you lied to and deceived me. Now I merely expect that you do as required with the least amount of fuss.'

'And does that include sleeping with you?' She laughed shrilly, tossing her head so that her hair floated around her shoulders, caught by the soft May breeze. She was wearing a fluffy white sweater with slim-fitting taupe trousers, an outfit which

should have been more than adequate for such
warm weather, yet she couldn't quite stem the cold
shudder that ran through her.

'If that is what I want, then the answer is yes.
You are my wife, Laura. Naturally I expect us to
share a bed and normal intimacies.'

'No!' Her eyes grew stormy with pain as the
memories rushed back. 'I will not subject myself
to a repeat of last night. It was vile, Luis!'

'Vile?' He raised one dark brow, his face calm
if one disregarded the growing darkness of his gaze.
'From what I recall, *adorada*, you seemed to enjoy
our lovemaking. Yet now you call it "vile"?' He
shook his head, the breeze ruffling his black hair
before he carelessly pushed it back. 'I wonder why
you are lying again. Or is it just that you are in-
capable of telling the truth?'

'It is the truth. I hated what you did to me!'

'So much so that you were like a wildcat, clawing
and biting at me?' He flicked the front of his shirt
open and drew it away from his shoulder, watching
her face as she saw the mark her teeth had left on
his tanned skin. He laughed softly, rebuttoning the
shirt as he held her shocked gaze. 'You wanted me,
Laura. You were with me every step of the way. I
didn't force you; I didn't have to. The desire you
feel for me and I feel for you was enough to ensure
that you made love with me willingly.'

'Love? Don't delude yourself, Luis. What we did
last night had nothing to do with love!'

'Maybe not, but it was still an enjoyable and
satisfying experience and one that I am sure we shall
both be eager to repeat many times over the next
few years. What bothers you most about it? The

fact that you think I tricked you in some way, or that you enjoyed having sex with me even though you profess to hate me so much?'

'I . . .'

'*Buenos días*, Luis . . . Laura.' The softly cultured tones of Doña Elena as she came out to join them on the terrace stopped Laura from replying. She swallowed down the hot retorts as Luis helped his mother into a chair. She had intended to be so composed for this first meeting with the other woman, but typically that wasn't to be.

She started nervously as she suddenly realised that Doña Elena was speaking to her. 'I'm sorry. I didn't catch that.'

The older woman smiled calmly, sitting erect in the chair. She was an imposing figure, her black hair sprinkled with silver and as immaculately arranged as ever, the elegant black suit she wore perfectly tailored to fit her slim figure. Laura had always found her stiff and unbending and it seemed that little about her attitude had changed.

'I merely enquired if you had slept well after your journey and all your recent exertions, Laura.'

'Exertions?' Laura repeated uncertainly, but it was Luis who explained.

'Nursing your friend, *querida*. Madre has been concerned that it might have been too much for you.' There was a touching warmth in his voice but it didn't fool her. This was all an act to convince his family of the lie he intended them to live.

Laura's eyes warred briefly with his but it was she who dropped her gaze first, unable to withstand the piercing scrutiny for long. 'I . . . fine, thank you.'

'I am glad to hear that. We were all beginning to worry that you were never coming back. Poor Luis has been left alone far too long. It is a good job that he is such an understanding husband, *sí?*'

'Yes.' Laura looked up and gave a stiff little smile as she carefully avoided Luis's eyes. 'He has been very... understanding.'

There was an undercurrent to the words she knew he had heard. She shot him a quick glance and felt her stomach clench at the anger which glittered briefly in his eyes before he laughed.

'There is a limit to how understanding a man can be and I had just about reached it, Laura. That is why I brought you home where you belong.' He stood up and stretched so that muscles rippled in his lean torso and despite herself, Laura felt her breath catch. He was such a devastatingly handsome man physically, that lean physique honed to perfection from all the sport he played, ranging from polo to skiing. He seemed to sense her reaction because he came round the table and held his hand out to her with a smile that made heat run along her veins even as her brain screamed a warning.

'Come, *querida*. I must change to go to the office, a necessity I regret but can do little about, I'm afraid. So let us enjoy a few minutes together before I leave.'

Conscious of Doña Elena watching them, Laura let him lead her inside, but once out of sight of the other woman she snatched her hand away from him. 'Very touching! And whose benefit was that for, Luis? Mine, or your mother's, more likely?'

He slid his hand under her elbow and ushered her quickly up the stairs to their room before he replied in a voice like steel, 'When will you learn a little discretion? I do not wish the servants to hear your shrew-like rantings!'

'Shrew-like? Why, you arrogant, insufferable...' She got no further, the words stopped abruptly as he pulled her into his arms and kissed her hard. He raised his head and studied her, watching the colour sweep up her face.

'Yes, shrew. And I find the prospect of taming you, little shrew, increasingly appealing.' His hand cupped her face. 'Perhaps that is why you act the way you do. Does the idea of being tamed excite you?'

'No!' She swatted his hands away and walked over to the window, keeping her back to him so that he couldn't see the heat in her face. She hated him for his cold arrogance but hated herself almost as much because there might be the smallest grain of truth in what he said. There *was* a certain heady excitement in pushing him to the limit and almost making his control snap, but why? Because deep down she still harboured some foolish hope that she might unleash other emotions inside him apart from hatred and this desire for revenge? Was she still crazy enough to hope for that after everything that had happened.

'It is a good job that the grapes aren't being harvested, Laura. You would sour the wine with that look.'

She turned on him in a trice, incensed by the mockery, then felt the words jam in her throat, held there by a sudden surge of raw desire. He had stripped off his shirt and was wearing only the tight-fitting breeches which hugged his narrow hips and muscular thighs. Sunlight gilded his chest, turning it the colour of bronze, each perfect muscle delineated. He looked like a sculpture standing there, so perfect yet so remote. He was her husband yet he felt nothing for her but hatred, and the pain she felt was so sharp that it was all she could do to hold back the cry of anguish.

'There is something wrong, Laura?'

She fought for control as Luis took a step towards her, terrified of letting him see how she felt. To give Luis that sort of advantage was asking for more heartache than she could cope with. 'No. Nothing at all. What did you want to speak to me about, or was that touching little episode downstairs purely for the benefit of your mother?'

His black brows drew together at the sarcasm, his tone holding a thread of steely anger. 'My mother has been unwell recently. I don't want her worrying about anything that can be avoided, do you understand? This marriage of ours is to appear perfect to everyone.'

'They would need to be blind to think that!'

'Not at all. Not if you play your part as adeptly as I know you are capable of. And after all, you do have such a fine incentive, don't you Laura? The thought of Rachel and her father homeless and penniless cannot be a pleasant one, not when you know it would be your fault?'

'My fault? That's the trouble, isn't it, Luis? I am to blame for all of it, according to you! Yet the only thing I am guilty of is loving you and imagining that you loved me back!'

Pain and anger made her grey eyes burn and she saw an answering flame ignite in Luis's dark ones. However, he controlled his anger and replied with a calmness which made her long to do something rash just to shake him, 'I have no intention of discussing that with you now, Laura. I have made my feelings plain enough for you to be in no doubt of them.'

'Well, bully for you! The great Luis de Rivera has spoken. How does it feel being so sure of yourself, Luis? Is it a good feeling, or does it sometimes get just the tiniest bit uncomfortable perched on top of that lofty pedestal? I only wish I were as perfect as you so obviously are!'

The words were hardly out of her mouth before he had her in his arms, his fingers bruising as they bit into her soft flesh. '*I* never claimed to be perfect.'

'Meaning that I did?' She tossed her head, the long glittering golden strands of hair swirling around her flushed face. Her heart was hammering, her pulse racing, her brain screaming out a warning to proceed with caution but all of a sudden caution was the last thing she intended to heed. 'I never lied to you, Luis! I never said one word to you to imply that I was a virgin!'

'No, you didn't.' He bent slightly, staring at her with eyes so dark they appeared almost lifeless. 'You were far too clever for that, my sweet wife, weren't you? You just convinced me of your innocence with your reluctance to allow our lovemaking to move beyond the purest of caresses, the chastest of kisses. You nearly drove me out of my mind wanting you the way I did and you knew it, didn't you? You knew exactly what you were doing just by letting me have the smallest taste of your delights so that I would be willing to go to any lengths to have all of you!'

'No! It wasn't like that. I was afraid. I told you that. I didn't try to trick or tease you into marriage. If anyone was tricked then it was me, Luis...me! I thought you loved me but obviously I was wrong!'

He let her go so abruptly she staggered, his face cold as he turned away to walk to the dressing-room. He paused in the doorway and she shrank away from the contempt on his face. 'There is no point in discussing this further. Apart from wanting to put mother's mind at rest I wanted you to know that I shall expect you to meet me for lunch today at the *bodega*.'

'Lunch?' She repeated the word automatically, her mind numb with pain. If only he had said something to deny the accusation, to let her believe that he had once loved her, but wishing for that was like wishing for the moon as he continued in the same cool, businesslike tone.

'Yes. I have a business meeting this morning with a buyer from a new supermarket chain which is interested in stocking our sherry. I thought it would be an advantage to have you join us for lunch to add a touch of informality to the meeting. I usually find that these people appreciate knowing that they warrant more than mere business courtesies.'

He sounded so cynical that she shivered. 'You really are cold and calculating. Do you ever do anything spontaneously, Luis? Or do you always plan each move beforehand so that you will come out on top?'

He shrugged. 'I merely try to cover all aspects. There is no room in business for sentiment, Laura. That was something my father taught me from an early age. A man sets out to accomplish things and achieves them by whichever means possible.'

'And it doesn't matter if he uses a little trickery?' She laughed bitterly. 'It's so different for you, isn't it, Luis? Is that something else your father impressed upon you, that the Riveras can do as they want without feeling any shame?'

'My father was a man of principle. He instilled those beliefs into me and I make no apologies now for the way I am. I take pride in the family name and I will allow nothing and no one to damage it. I shall expect you at one o'clock. Get José to drive you into town.'

He turned to carry on into the dressing-room, barely breaking stride when Laura said softly, 'What a shame that your father didn't impress upon you that it is necessary to forgive others for mistakes they make by being not quite as perfect as you, Luis.'

If he heard her he gave no sign, closing the door quietly behind him. Laura slowly turned to go, knowing it was futile to remain there. Luis would run his life and hers along the lines he chose to and there was little she could do to stop him. But somehow she had to find a way to make him listen to her even if he would never accept what she told him. She couldn't bear the thought of living the rest of her life like this.

* * *

The shoes had been a mistake. Pale cream leather with three-inch heels, they matched her cream dress perfectly and lent a touch of elegant height to her five-foot, five-inch frame. Now, however, half a mile from town and an equal distance from the *casa*, Laura knew they had been a mistake. Unless the real mistake lay in her decision to walk into town and not ask José to drive her to the lunch appointment.

Fanning herself with her cream leather bag, she struggled on and tried not to think about how annoyed Luis was going to be when she arrived so late for the appointment. But there was no denying the swift alarm she felt when a familiar car screeched to a halt on the opposite side of the road before performing a rapid turn to draw up alongside her.

'Get in.'

There was anger in every grim line of Luis's face and laced through the curt order but Laura refused to bow down before it. 'No, thank you. I prefer to walk rather than suffer your company in that sort of a mood.'

'*Madre de Dios*! You would try the patience of a saint! Now get in before I make you.' His anger was rising, warning her that his patience was indeed tried to the limit. Without another word she climbed into the car, staring straight ahead as Luis put it into gear and shot towards the town.

'And what did you hope to achieve by this?' He barely glanced at her, his hands busy on the wheel as he steered the powerful car through the increasingly heavy traffic with all the flair and skill he did everything.

Laura shrugged, surreptitiously easing the shoes off. 'Nothing. I just felt like a walk that's all.'

'All?' Anger exploded from him as he slowed the car to a stop and turned to glare at her. 'It was a foolish and thoughtless thing to do. Did it never occur to you to tell anyone where you were going? Mother has been most concerned since I phoned and discovered that you were apparently missing.'

'I never meant to upset her. She knew I was lunching with you so I just assumed she would know that was where I had gone. I just wanted to be by myself for a while.'

'And did you give no thought to what might have happened to you, wandering about all alone? *Dios*, Laura, even you cannot be so stupid that you don't realise you could have been putting yourself at risk!' He caught her by the shoulders and gave her a hard shake.

'Obviously nothing did happen, did it? I am perfectly all right if you discount the bruises you are inflicting on me.' She shrugged out of his hold, hating the way he was treating her like some sort of imbecile rather than a grown woman.

'I should do more than shake you!' He slammed a hand on the steering-wheel and suddenly Laura knew she'd had enough. This scene on top of everything else that had happened was more than she could cope with. She gave a brilliant smile, her voice like glass when she spoke.

'Carry on like this, darling, and I shall start thinking that you were worried about me,' she taunted.

'I was.' He paused, studying her for a long moment before he smiled with a chilling contempt.

'I was worried that your tardiness would ruin what promises to be a very successful business meeting. Now shall we carry on? I have wasted enough time already.'

He started the engine and Laura turned away to hide her tears at his cruelty. It had been deliberate, she knew, yet another strike against her in his search for revenge, but even knowing it didn't stop the pain.

Lunch was less of an ordeal than she'd feared. Luis had slipped back once more into the smoothly urbane guise of businessman, leading the conversation at the table with his usual panache and sophistication, aided by Miguel Moreno who handled the firm's foreign contracts.

A man in his late fifties, Miguel had been with the firm for many years, working formerly for Luis's father. He was a shrewd and well respected businessman yet Laura couldn't help but notice that he treated Luis with a marked deference. It wasn't just that Luis was head of the company now but because Miguel, along with many others, had come to respect Luis for his abilities.

Laura had only a sketchy knowledge of the Rivera family history but, from what she had learned, knew that, since Luis had taken over on the death of his father six years before, the firm had gone from strength to strength. He had been only twenty-four at the time but his foresight and determination had made the company what it was today, one of the front runners in a highly competitive market. Single-mindedness had taken him to the top, that same single-mindedness that was set to ruin both their lives.

That thought weighed heavily on her, making it difficult for her to join in the conversation, and she saw Luis shoot her an irritated glance. She glared back at him then felt her heart sink when a familiar voice suddenly intruded on the conversation.

'Luis, I didn't know you were lunching here today. You should have told me so that we could have made arrangements to meet up.'

Mercedes stopped by the table, immaculate as ever in an elegant white dress. She smiled when Luis stood up and kissed her on both cheeks, her gaze skimming the other occupants of the table as the two men gallantly rose to their feet.

'A business meeting, Mercedes, as you can see, otherwise we would have been delighted to have you join us. Isn't that so, Laura?'

Laura managed to murmur something polite but it was hard to hide her dislike of the other woman. She averted her eyes when Mercedes drew Luis to one side to whisper something to him in a confiding tone then laughed with a husky familiarity that grated on every nerve in Laura's body.

'Pay no attention to my sister, Laura. She doesn't mean any harm, really.'

Laura jumped, shooting an uncertain glance over her shoulder at the man standing behind her chair. He smiled broadly, drawing over a chair from an empty table nearby to sit down beside her. 'I'm Domingo... remember? Mercedes's brother.'

Laura blushed uncomfortably. 'Oh. I'm sorry but I'm afraid I didn't recognise you for a moment. How are you?'

'Fine thank you. And even more so for meeting you again like this.' His dark eyes studied her face with undisguised admiration which was like balm after Luis's coldness. Laura smiled with a touch of warmth. She had only met Domingo once before at a party given for her and Luis when they had announced that they were to be married, and then had spoken to him only briefly, too concerned with making sure she didn't say the wrong thing.

'That sounds to me like well practised flattery,' she chided with a small laugh.

Domingo smiled back, his handsome face exuding a boyish charm which Laura knew from gossip had conquered more than one susceptible female heart. He was a few years younger than her, she guessed, but in experience with the opposite sex many years her senior. However, there was no way she could object when he continued to pay her a string of ludicrously fulsome compliments, ignoring her laughing protests.

'I hate to break up your talk, Laura, but it is time Domingo and I joined our party.' Mercedes' voice was smooth but there was no way that Laura could miss the edge to it as she continued. 'I hope you will accompany Luis to the polo match tomorrow. You and Domingo seem to be getting along so well that I am sure you will be good company for each other.'

'We shall be there, Mercedes. We shall look forward to seeing you and Domingo then.'

Luis's tone was bland but Laura could see the flash of anger in his eyes as Domingo got up and kissed her hand with heavy gallantry. When the pair had gone, she tried to push the incident to the back of her mind, but every time she met Luis's eyes she could see the annoyance still lingering there.

When the meeting finally broke up, he took her arm and led her back to the *bodega*, putting her into his car and driving back to the *casa* without a word. Laura's nerves were raw by the time they pulled up in the driveway, the tension making her feel sick. When Luis helped her out she hung back but he was ruthless as he led her inside and up to their room, closing the door and leaning against it in a way that sent alarm skittering through her.

'Well, Laura? What do you have to say for yourself?'

'I . . . I don't know what you mean.' She stared at him with huge grey eyes. 'Why are you acting like this, Luis?'

'You ask me that after your performance in the restaurant?' His anger was suddenly unleashed, cold and icy rather than hot, and somehow more terrible because of it.

'What performance? I . . . I did my best to be pleasant to the buyer. I don't understand!'

'Don't you? Once I might have believed you, but one thing you aren't, sweet Laura, is naïve or innocent!' He stepped towards her, towering over her now. 'You made a spectacle of yourself, laughing and simpering with Domingo like some young girl. I will not tolerate such behaviour from my wife. You will act in a manner that befits your position in future!'

'You have the nerve to say that!' Anger was a blessing. It chased away the hurt, the fear. 'You accuse me of making a spectacle of myself after the way you and Mercedes were whispering together like . . . like lovers! But then that's probably what you are, isn't that so, Luis? But don't you dare take that high-handed attitude with me when you are at fault!'

She pushed past him, refusing to listen to such hypocrisy a moment longer, but he caught her around the waist and pulled her to him.

'We were not discussing my behaviour, Laura, but yours. You are my wife.'

'And you are supposed to be my husband...whatever that means!' she spat back at him.

'Oh, I know all right, even though it had been so long since you played the role of wife until yesterday.' His voice had dropped, rough velvet now rather than steel, and she shivered in response to it then saw the very instant when his anger took on a new, shocking direction.

'Luis, I...' She stopped abruptly, her breath catching as he drew her closer, easing her hips into intimate contact with his.

'You...what, Laura? Want to show me how well you play your role? Want me to show you how I can be a husband?' His hands slid down her back, curving round her buttocks as he moved her against him.

'No! Stop it, Luis! Stop it.' She tried to drag his hands away from her then gasped when he captured hers and held them behind her back, curving her even more closely to him so that she could be left in no doubt at all as to his intentions. When he bent to kiss her, she turned her head sharply, willing herself to fight him every step of the way but it was far more difficult than she could have imagined as he let his mouth run along the line of her jaw, the curve of her cheek before he traced the delicate curl of her ear with his tongue.

Laura shuddered violently as the fire that had started with the first touch of his mouth spread through her whole body. She didn't want to feel this wild desire, this longing, but she seemed not to have the strength to fight against it.

Incoherent little murmurs of sound mingled with the rasp of his breathing as they waged a silent battle, a battle not of blows but of caresses. His mouth seemed to be made of gossamer as it skimmed her skin, brushing kisses over every sensitive inch yet it left behind a trail of havoc. Fire burned in its wake, licking along her nerves, stirring her senses until she was almost mindless with the desire he had ignited inside her. When his mouth finally came to rest on hers she was lost.

Late afternoon sun streamed in the window, gleaming on their sweat-slicked limbs as they made love with a fervent need in the middle of the huge bed. Luis never spoke, whispered no words of encouragement or endearment, and neither did she. They didn't need words, just the feel of each other's body under hands that caressed, mouths that sought. It was the most elemental of couplings yet it seemed to transcend time and space, carrying them to another world as they drove each other to the brink of fulfilment and beyond.

It seemed to take forever for her breathing to slow, for the deep shudders to ease. Laura lay quite still, watching the sunlight reflected on the carved ceiling while she stroked her hand down Luis's back, loving the feel of his skin under her fingers. His breathing was gradually slowing, his heartbeat steadying as he too returned from passion's clutches and suddenly she knew that now was the time to admit to him something she had finally admitted to herself during those last frantic moments as heaven had lain within their grasp. She loved him. She always had, she always would. It was his right to know.

'Luis, I want to tell you something.' Her voice was soft but there was no hesitancy in it. She wanted to tell him how she felt because somehow she knew it would make a huge difference to them.

'What is it?' He rolled over and stood up, stretching his muscles, arrogant and so gloriously male that Laura felt the tremors start to flare up again inside her. He must have sensed her reaction because he smiled with just the faintest hint of cynicism as he dropped down to sit beside her on the bed and run a finger down the curve of her breast.

Laura bit back a gasp, colour touching her cheeks as he smiled and did it again before letting his hand drop to the bed in a careless little gesture that left her feeling somehow bereft.

'So what are you going to tell me, *amada*? That you love me?' He must have seen the shock in her eyes because his smile deepened despite the fact that his own eyes were suddenly cold.

Laura fought down the fear, staring back at him. 'Yes, I do, Luis. I love you.'

For words that she had wanted to say they seemed to be strangely difficult to utter now as she stared into those cold eyes. 'Don't...don't you believe me?'

'Of course.' He stood up again and walked towards the dressing-room, leaving her staring after him. But there was no way she could let him go like this.

'Luis! Doesn't it mean anything to you?' She was shaking so hard that it was hard to force the words out, watching with wide, shocked eyes as he stopped halfway across the room to glance back, and she felt something inside her die at the expression of indifference on his face.

'Frankly, Laura, no. It doesn't matter to me one bit what you feel.'

If he had struck her it couldn't have been such a cruel blow. Laura sank back on the bed, unable to speak as Luis left the room. Words or even tears weren't enough to ease such utter desolation. All she could think of was all the long years to come, living with a man who cared so little about her that he was indifferent to her love.

CHAPTER FIVE

THE sound of horses galloping across the dry earth
mixed with the shouts of their riders. Laura sat
under a tree, looking towards the polo field without
really following what was happening. Somewhere
among the men who were racing their ponies across
the grass in pursuit of the ball was Luis, leading
his team to yet another victory, but she could take
no pleasure from the thought.

Suddenly a great roar went up as he scored
another goal for his team. He raised his stick in
acknowledgement then galloped his pony back
across the field, his concentration once more
centred on the game. He had a handicap of nine,
just one short of the very top players, and was a
ruthless competitor in a sport which his family had
played for many years. Polo for Luis was not just
a game. It was a test of skill and determination and
sometimes mind-boggling risk which Laura had
never been able to understand the justification for.
However, Luis had never seen it her way, laughing
off her fears, and now he didn't care one way or
the other what her views were.

Pain was a hard lump of ice in her chest. It had
settled there the previous evening when Luis had
walked out of the bedroom and nothing seemed to
be able to melt it away. Now, feeling the tears
welling in her eyes, Laura stood up and left the
crowd, wanting to be by herself to regain her com-

posure. Luis might not care how she felt, but there was no way that she was going to put her emotions on display for onlookers. She'd been painfully aware of the interest her arrival had caused as Luis had escorted her across the field before leaving her to change for the match. If pride was all she had left then she would cling to it like a life-raft rather than sink in that sea of gossip and speculation. Pain as sharp and bitter as she felt now couldn't last, and she would hold on to that thought to see her through.

'Laura? Are you all right?'

She stopped when a hand caught her by the arm, forcing a bright smile for the man who was studying her with some concern. 'Of course. I'm sorry, Domingo. I was miles away just now. I never even noticed you.'

He laughed, pushing a hand into the pocket of his tight white breeches. 'What a blow to a man's ego.'

Laura laughed at the wryness, stepping aside as two women she recognised as being friends of Mercedes tried to pass them on the narrow path. They murmured a greeting to her then put their heads together as soon as they were past, obviously making some sort of comment about her. Laura sighed heavily, hating to be the butt of gossip, but Luis was so well known in the town that it was only to be expected that people should speculate about her prolonged absence.

Domingo glanced after the two women then turned back to her. 'Your presence here seems to be exciting a great deal of comment.'

'I'm sure it is, but there is little I can do about it, so there is no point in my worrying.'

He didn't seem deterred by the cool note in her voice. 'It is rather odd, though.'

'Is it?' Laura glanced past him, wishing she could find some way to put an end to this conversation.

'You must know it is. You'd been married barely a few months then suddenly you disappeared. It seemed a strange thing for a new bride to do, and a strange thing for Luis to allow you to do.'

'Luis has been...understanding about it all,' she said quietly, feeling the pain tightening in her chest.

'He has. I must say that I wouldn't have been happy to let you go back to England and stay for such a long time, Laura, despite your having the most altruistic reason for doing so. I would have wanted you by my side.'

Domingo's voice had taken on an intimate note she didn't feel comfortable with. When he took her arm and started to walk along the path with her, she glanced uncertainly back over her shoulder. 'Shouldn't you be getting back to the game?'

He shrugged lightly. 'I have played once today. That is enough. I don't have Luis's dedication. There is a lot more to life than hurling oneself around the polo field.'

There was little she could say to argue with that train of thought so Laura walked with him, stopping when they reached a shady patch of trees to beg a respite from the heat. She leant against a thick tree-trunk, hearing the faint sounds of the game continuing in the distance.

'Is there something wrong between you and Luis, Laura?'

She jumped when Domingo asked the question. 'Of course not! What makes you think that there is?'

'Mercedes,' he said bluntly. He leant a shoulder against the tree-trunk beside her, his handsome face filled with curiosity. 'And she has always been close to Luis. Everyone thought that they would marry before you came along.'

And perhaps they should have, Laura thought fleetingly. If she had never married Luis then she wouldn't be going through all this heartache now. However, there was no way she dared let Domingo know her feelings. Luis would be furious if he heard any hint that his plans weren't working out. She had to find some way to allay the curiosity she could see on Domingo's handsome face.

'Well, I'm happy to say that Mercedes is quite wrong in this instance. Luis and I are very happy together.' She shrugged lightly, forcing a warm little smile. 'Oh, it isn't all roses, of course, but which marriage is? And we've had to contend not only with this separation but the fact that our two lives have been so different up to now. My background is vastly different from Luis's, but then they always say that opposites attract.'

'You were a teacher before you married, I believe?' Some of the avid curiosity had faded from Domingo's eyes as he relaxed against the tree-trunk, and Laura felt some of the tension ease.

'Mmm, that's right. I enjoyed it, although it was hard work. I was planning on going back to it once

I returned from the trip around Europe but of course I met Luis.'

'Was it something you always wanted to do?'

She laughed. 'My mother was a teacher, and my father, so I guess you could call it a family calling. It was always in the back of my mind that I would go in for it as well. Then when my mother died when I was in my teens it decided it for me. I suppose I wanted to follow in her footsteps, and I've never regretted the decision.'

'Then maybe your background isn't that different from Luis's after all.' He saw her surprise and smiled. 'It is a tradition in Spanish families that children follow in their parents' footsteps. There was never any doubt that Luis would take over from his father and run the business, extremely well by all accounts.'

'And what about you, Domingo? Will you take over from your father?'

'Probably.' He shrugged carelessly. 'Unfortunately I do not have Luis's drive and single-mindedness. He has lived, breathed and dreamed of the *bodega* for years! I prefer to enjoy life a little more.' He laughed. 'In fact, I imagine that Mercedes would be better suited to running the company if our father ever retires but, as the son, it is expected that I shall step into his shoes.'

Which only served to highlight once again just how suited Mercedes would have been to the role of Luis's wife. Laura swallowed down the sudden stab of pain and fixed a determined smile to her face.

'Well, pleasant though it has been talking to you, I really must get back. Luis will be wondering where I have got to if the game has finished.'

'Will he?' Domingo gave a wicked smile. 'I imagine that my sister will do her best to keep him company.'

There was little that Laura could say so she ignored the comment and started briskly up the path again, her footsteps slowing as the polo field came into sight. There seemed to be a great deal of activity around the perimeter and then the wail of an ambulance siren cut through the air.

Without really understanding why, she started to run, her heart thumping in fear as she reached the group Luis had introduced her to earlier. There was no sign of him, nor could she see him among the group of players leading their ponies from the field.

'Where is Luis? Has something happened?' she demanded, but it wasn't until Domingo spoke rapidly to them in Spanish that she had her answer.

He turned to her at once, his face very grave. 'There has been an accident. Luis and a member of the opposing team crashed into one another and their ponies fell.'

'Is he hurt?' Shock echoed in the husky sound of her voice.

'Yes, but not too badly from what I've been told. The other rider has been taken to hospital but Luis has gone home. Come, Laura, I shall drive you there.'

She was glad of Domingo's help as he led the way to the car, curbing her impatience when several people stopped them along the way. All she wanted was to get back to the house to see for herself how bad Luis was. When the car stopped, she jumped out and rushed inside, pausing when she found Luis's mother in the hall.

'How is he? Is he badly hurt? Where is he now?'

'He is upstairs with the doctor. We shall have to wait until after he has finished his examination to learn how bad the injuries are.' Doña Elena's voice was cold. 'Mercedes drove him back when you could not be found.'

Laura barely registered the condemnation in the older woman's voice. 'I shall go up and see how he is.'

She ran up the stairs, feeling herself go weak with relief when she found Luis seated in a chair in their bedroom while the doctor strapped his shoulder with a heavy crêpe bandage. He glanced round as she came into the room but there was little welcome in his eyes.

'How do you feel?' She waited until the doctor had finished and gone into the bathroom to wash his hands.

'How do you imagine I feel? It was a bad fall but I fared better than the other rider. But of course you didn't see it, did you? You were too busy elsewhere.'

'I had gone for a walk. I didn't know that it was going to happen. No one could have known!' She was instantly on the defensive, hating to hear that harsh note in his voice. The trouble was that her nerves were ready to snap, this incident, coming on top of yesterday's, too much.

All night long she had brooded about Luis's cruelty, claiming a headache to avoid having to dine with him and Doña Elena. But the tension had grown as the hours had passed and night had fallen. The thought of having Luis make love to her again after what he'd said was almost more than she could bear as was the stark realisation that she wasn't confident of resisting his advances. He might have dismissed her love with a chilling disregard but that didn't mean it changed how she felt about him.

She started when Luis spoke again, her eyes shadowed as they searched his unforgiving face. 'Perhaps not, but I did not expect that you would deliberately flout my wishes, not after yesterday. Arranging to meet Domingo was foolish in the extreme.'

'I met him by accident. It wasn't...' She broke off as a knock sounded at the door.

Mercedes came into the room, a bright smile on her full lips. 'Ahhh, Laura. You managed to get here at last. I did try to find you but you and Domingo must have tucked yourselves away somewhere secluded.' She shrugged delicately, her meaning more than apparent. She was doing it deliberately, trying to push a wedge between them, and succeeding.

Laura's temper rose but before she could say anything the doctor reappeared. He handed Luis a small vial of tablets from his bag with a few murmured instructions then left.

'As you are here now, Laura, I think it is time I left.' Mercedes walked over to Luis and bent to kiss his cheek. 'If you need me for anything, Luis, just call.'

'Thank you. You have done enough today, Mercedes, more than enough.' Luis smiled at the woman in a way which made Laura's heart almost tear itself to shreds with jealousy. He never looked at her that way any longer, not with that warmth. Something of what she felt must have shown because Mercedes's eyes reflected satisfaction as the woman glanced at her before turning back to Luis again.

'It was only what any... friend would have done, Luis.'

Every drop of colour faded from Laura's face at the deliberate taunt. She stayed silent until Mercedes left then turned to Luis. 'I will not be humiliated like that, Luis!'

'I have no idea what you mean.' His voice was cold, his expression one of pure arrogance as he stood up. He seemed to sway for a moment before he caught his balance but Laura could see the effort it cost him from the way his jaw tightened. Forgetting her outrage for a moment, she hurried to him and slid an arm around his lean waist to steady him.

'Decided to play the dutiful wife now, Laura?' There was mockery in that deep velvet voice but it was overlaid by weariness and echoes of pain, and she bit back the hot retort.

'You're hurt, Luis. You need help. What did the doctor say? Why is your shoulder bandaged?'

He smiled faintly at the soft enquiry but answered levelly. 'A dislocated shoulder. He has put it back in place and the bandage will keep it there until it starts to heal.'

'Why do you take such risks?' She couldn't help the question, her grey eyes clouded at the thought of the pain he must have suffered and indeed must still be suffering.

'Life is a risk, Laura. Every thing we do from the cradle to the grave holds some kind of a risk. One makes a choice, chooses a route, then all that is left is to live with the consequences.'

In a sudden flash of insight she knew that he wasn't just talking about the risks of playing the sport. He was talking about their marriage and the bitter consequences they must both suffer for the course they had each chosen towards it. Luis must regret ever taking her as his wife, the same as she regretted not telling him about that one episode from her past that lay between them, an obstacle that could never be overcome, it seemed.

When he moved away from her to go and lie down on the bed she made no attempt to help him. He didn't want her help or her concern or her love. All she was to him now was the consequence of an act he bitterly regretted.

The moon was a pale patch of luminescence against the ink-dark sky. Laura stepped out on to the terrace, closing the door quietly behind her. A soft breeze was blowing, carrying on it the night-rich scent of the tubs of flowers overlaid by the faint tang of the vines which stretched acre upon acre away from the house. In another few weeks the air would be redolent with the smell of the ripening fruit but for now it was just a faint promise of the harvest to come.

Sitting down on one of the white iron chairs by the table, she rested her head back as she studied the clear, dark sky. It was already quite late but she didn't feel tired, too keyed up with tension to relax. She had been by herself all evening long since Doña

Elena had left to dine at a friend's house but she hadn't missed having her company. Luis had asked for a tray to be sent to his room and eaten there, leaving Laura the sole occupant of the huge dining-room with its massive, polished oak table. She had sat in solitary state, doing her best to show her appreciation of the exquisite meal which had been served to her with all the customary formality. What would the servants have said if she'd suddenly announced a desire to eat in the kitchen with them, she mused. They would have probably been just as shocked as Luis and his mother by such bizarre behaviour.

A faint, almost whimsical smile curved her mouth as she got up and walked over to the edge of the terrace, taking the steps to the path which led around the house. The Casa de Flores was built in traditional Spanish style around a central courtyard but there had been a few additions made over the years. Now, as she came to the walled area that sheltered the swimming pool from any curious eyes, Laura found herself following the path to the side of the pool. She glanced down at the deep azure water, watching the way the breeze curled tiny ripples across its surface, feeling the restlessness increasing. She had to do something to work it off otherwise she would never be able to sleep tonight, and what better way than to swim a few laps of the pool?

Without another thought, she kicked off her shoes and unzipped the back of her navy silk dress, draping it carefully over a nearby lounge chair. She glanced round uncertainly but there was no one in sight. The pool area was far enough away from the

main house to be left in darkness, the moon the
only source of light.

Reassured, she slipped off her bra and panties
then slid into the water, gasping as the coldness
sluiced over her warm skin. A shiver ran through
her and determinedly she ducked fully under the
water then set off at a brisk pace to swim several
lengths before sheer exhaustion called a halt. She
rolled over to float on her back, watching the sky
drift past in a hazy mist of silver stars.

'You will catch cold at this time of the year if
you stay in there too long.'

The shock of hearing Luis's voice was so great
that she sank beneath the water and came up splut-
tering. Rubbing the stinging drops from her eyes,
she searched the perimeter of the pool until she
finally spotted him seated in a chair on the far side.

'I...I didn't know you were there,' she said
inanely.

'There seemed little reason to announce my
presence and spoil your pleasure, *querida*.' His teeth
gleamed white as he smiled. 'And if you had realised
that I was here I doubt you would have put on that
charming little display.'

Her face flamed at the thought of exactly what
he must have seen as she'd stood naked on the edge
of the pool for a moment before diving into the
water. 'It would have been good manners to make
me aware of your presence, Luis. That would have
been something a true gentleman would have done!'

He ignored the bite in her tone, his laughter
carrying easily to her ears. 'Mmm. I'm sure you
are right. But sometimes being a "gentleman" can

be inhibiting. One can miss out on all sorts of delightful pleasures.'

She wasn't sure if it was what he said or the way that he said it which disturbed her most, and as he suddenly stood up and walked over to the pool she had no time to decide. She backed away from the edge, sinking deeper into the water, all too conscious of her nakedness. When Luis suddenly dropped down to crouch on the edge, her heart skipped a beat and she searched for something to say to break the sudden tension that seemed to flow between them.

'Don't you think you should be inside resting your shoulder?'

He shrugged then grimaced as the movement made his injured shoulder hurt. 'I am tired of resting. I am not an old man yet, Laura, who needs hours upon hours of rest to recover from an injury. In a few days it will be good as new...if I can survive the boredom such a restriction places upon me.'

He wasn't old by any means. Her eyes took a hurried stocktake of his lean torso partly exposed by the shirt he'd drawn on but had to leave unbuttoned over the thick bandages. In the moonlight his skin looked dark against the whiteness of the crêpe, smooth as satin. She wanted to reach out and run her fingers across it just to savour the feel but that was a foolish, crazy idea, of course.

'You still shouldn't overdo things, Luis.' Her voice held a huskiness she knew at once he had heard and understood.

'No?' He shifted slightly in his crouched position, steadying himself with one hand on the tiled floor. The action opened the front of the shirt even more, giving her glimpses of his strong stomach muscles, and she felt a sudden heat curl inside her. Deliberately she turned and swam to the far side of the pool then stopped uncertainly as she realised her dilemma. Her clothes were still lying on the chair close to where Luis was now standing watching her. Even if she climbed out at this side she would still have to go back to collect them. She couldn't walk back to the house without a stitch on!

'Your concern for my well-being is touching, *amada*. It only heightens my concern for you. Isn't it time you got out before you catch a chill?'

'I'm fine. I think I'll just do another few laps. Don't bother to wait for me to finish, Luis. You go on back to the house.' She set off swimming again but by the time she had swum another four laps of the pool he was still there. She stopped at the far side to catch her breath, feeling her legs trembling with the unaccustomed exercise. Her knees felt like rubber, her arms aching; there was no way she could swim any more yet no way she could climb out with Luis standing there watching her.

'Finished now, *querida*?' There was warm amusement in his deep voice. It lit the first spark of anger inside her.

'Yes!'

'Then it is time to get out.'

'I have no intention of getting out while you are standing there!' Now that she had stopped swimming she could feel a chill invading her limbs and her teeth chattered quite audibly.

'I have seen you naked many times, Laura. What difference does one more time make to you?'

She had no idea, but it did! A whole lot of difference, in fact. 'I am not getting out while you are there. Understand?'

'I do.' He turned away and she gave a tiny sigh of relief that was short-lived when he merely sat down on one of the chairs.

'Luis!'

'Sí. You want something, *amada*?'

'I want you to leave, but I suppose that is too much to expect!'

'How can I possibly leave you by yourself? You could slip and hurt yourself. Anything could happen, and I would never forgive myself, Laura.'

'I imagine it would serve your purpose if something did happen to me! Then you would have me out of your life for good!'

That first spark had started a fire but surprisingly Luis merely laughed at her anger. He got up and walked around the pool, stopping beside her to offer her his hand. 'You are getting angry because you are cold and uncomfortable. Come along, Laura, be sensible.'

It was obvious that he wouldn't give in and just as obvious that she couldn't stay in the water any longer. Her whole body was already so numb that she could barely feel her legs.

With a glare in Luis's direction she ignored his hand and hauled herself out of the water then found to her chagrin that her legs just wouldn't support her. She stumbled forward and heard Luis mutter something under his breath which she took to be an oath before his arm went around her, drawing her against him for support.

'Little fool. You are always so determined to do things your way rather than see sense.'

She didn't appreciate that assessment but could do little about it as the weakness spread through her limbs. When Luis drew her closer to him, taking her weight, she murmured a protest before falling silent. It felt so good to have him hold her like this, to feel the warmth of his body against her. If she closed her eyes then she could pretend that everything was all right again, that he still loved her as she loved him.

'Come. The night air is cool. Go and put your clothes back on.'

The curt instruction brought reality back with a jolt that was painful. She moved away from him at once, wrapping her arms around her trembling body as she hurried to where she had left her clothes and dragged them on over her wet skin, but even then it was difficult to stop the shivers which racked her.

'*Dios*, Laura! You will be lucky to escape a severe chill after this folly.' Anger was a thread of steel in his voice. It startled her into looking round at him and she felt the shudders intensify as she saw him watching her. The moon chose that moment to slide silently from behind a cloud, lighting his tall, imposing figure in its stark silver glow. Luis had always exuded an urbane sophistication which stemmed from both his wealth and his background, yet he looked so different from the man she knew as he stood there, legs slightly apart, the white shirt hanging open over his tanned chest with its heavy strapping of bandages. He looked almost primitive like that, and it shocked her.

She must have made some sound, although she wasn't conscious of doing so. It seemed to draw him back from the edge of some deep emotion and as she watched his face settled back into its customary lines.

'You need to get warm. Come inside at once and I shall make you a drink.' He made no attempt to touch her as he walked past her to the house. If she hadn't had that fleeting glimpse of him in the moonlight then she would never have seen that unexpected change in him. What had he been thinking, feeling just now? She wished she knew, wished that for once in his life he would let the barriers fall and allow her to get close to him. But that was like wishing for that huge silver moon to drop at her feet, because it would never happen.

CHAPTER SIX

THE house was quiet when they went back inside. Laura was surprised to find that it was after midnight when she glanced at the ornate clock hanging on the wall in the hall. She hadn't realised how long she'd been outside, nor how long she must have spent in the pool. No wonder she was so cold and numb.

She followed Luis across the hall, then stopped when he opened the door to his study and beckoned her inside. He raised a mocking brow when she stood hesitating by the stairs. 'I will give you some brandy to warm that chill from your body.'

'I...I don't really need anything, thank you.' She forced herself to stand quite still but it was impossible to hide the shiver that raced through her, and he smiled.

'There is no need to worry. Brandy is all I have on my mind, so come along inside.'

His mockery annoyed her and she marched towards the door, refusing to let him think that she was afraid. However, Luis barely glanced at her as he closed the door then went and poured two generous measures of brandy into balloon glasses, carrying them back to where she was still standing just inside the room.

'Please sit down. You will feel far more comfortable, I am sure, rather than standing there as though you are half tempted to run away at the first move I make. You are quite safe, *querida*. Even if I were so inclined I doubt I am up to forcing myself upon you in this state.'

Did he really imagine that she was going to stand there and be taunted like that? With a mutter of annoyance, she pushed past him, forgetful of his injured shoulder until she heard the sharp hiss of his breath and saw all the colour drain from his face. 'Are you all right? Luis?'

She lifted the glasses from his hands and set them down on the table by the couch then watched helplessly as he sank down on to it, his lips rimmed with white.

'I . . . have . . . felt better.' His voice was rough, belying the dismissive statement and she dropped to her knees in front of him.

'I'm so sorry, Luis. I never meant to do that. Can I get you anything? Or shall I call the doctor?' She started to scramble to her feet but he stopped her with a hand on her arm.

'No. There is no need for that. On the table in my dressing-room . . . you will find some pain-relief tablets that the doctor left for me.'

'I'll fetch them at once. Stay there and don't move.' She ran from the room and up the stairs, finding the bottle exactly where he had said. Clutching it tightly, she ran back downstairs then hesitated outside the study before running across the hall to the kitchen to fill a glass with water.

'Here you are. How many are you supposed to take?' Flipping the cap on the bottle, she shook a few tablets into her hand then stared worriedly at the instructions printed in Spanish on the white label. From what she could tell it said that he could take two, but how often and with what sort of a time-lapse between dosages?

'Just give me one. That will be sufficient. I don't want to become dependent on drugs!' There was a rough impatience in his voice as he held his hand out while she dropped a single tablet into it and her eyes narrowed suspiciously.

'How many did the doctor tell you to take, and how many times a day?' she asked quietly as she handed him the glass of water and watched him swallow the tablet with a grimace of distaste.

He cast her a cool look, running a hand over the bandage as he settled more comfortably against the cushions. 'I can see no reason to take them on a regular basis. They will not heal the torn muscles, merely mask the pain.'

'Then surely that is the best reason in the world to take them! Really, Luis, it is ridiculous to try to do without pain-killers when you need them.'

He smiled faintly, resting his dark head back as he stared up at her through narrowed eyes. 'Does the idea of my suffering upset you, Laura? I should have imagined that you would feel glad that I had been punished in this way for making you come back here with me.'

'I don't want to see you in pain! What a horrible thing to say.'

'Was it? Then I apologise. I keep forgetting that you still profess to have some feelings left for me despite everything that has happened.' He laughed as she turned her face away. 'Why does it upset you to hear me remind you of that? Yesterday you were only too anxious to tell me how you felt.'

'And yesterday you made it quite clear that you weren't interested, one way or another!' She took a deep breath, refusing to let the pain cloud her mind to what he was doing. Luis seemed to take a great pleasure from taunting her this way but if she was to survive then she would have to learn to hide just how successful he was with his gibes. 'However, what happened yesterday is not under discussion here. Do you want me to get you anything else before I go upstairs to bed?'

It took a moment before he answered, and just fleetingly she caught a glimpse of something akin to admiration in his eyes before it disappeared so fast that she knew she must have imagined seeing it. 'I would like some coffee if it isn't too much trouble. I don't think it would be wise to drink the brandy on top of that tablet.'

'It most certainly wouldn't. I shall go and make some for you.'

Glad of the breathing space, she hurried to the kitchen and filled the coffeemaker then glanced at her reflection in the darkened window. Her hair was straggling around her shoulders, her silk dress sticking limply to her after being dragged on before. It would take a few minutes for the coffee to drip so she might as well go and change into something comfortable while she waited.

It took only minutes to slip off the crumpled clothes and towel her hair dry. She slid on a dainty pale green cotton nightshirt which skimmed her thighs then covered it with a thick fleecy white towelling robe. Her hair was almost dry but curling wildly about her face after the brusque handling so she brushed it back and tied it up high on her head with a length of white ribbon. Then, feeling far more like herself, she ran back down to the kitchen, stopping abruptly when she found Luis there.

He glanced round when he heard her, his dark eyes skimming her slender figure in the warm, thick robe, then turned back to pouring coffee into two heavy white mugs. 'Do you still take cream and sugar?'

'Er—yes, but you shouldn't have bothered. I would have finished making the coffee.' She moved uncertainly just one step further into the room, wondering why she felt suddenly nervous. Nothing had changed, Luis still looked his usual self, fully in control, yet she could sense a certain change in the atmosphere, unless it was just her mind playing tricks.

'It was no trouble, and you need this as much as I do, Laura.' His voice was soft and throbbingly vibrant. It seemed to ripple across the room towards her, stirring her senses.

'I...I do?' she queried huskily.

'Mmm, of course. You must still be cold after that swim.'

He was wrong about that; she wasn't cold, in fact, she was starting to feel uncomfortably warm. There was something disturbingly intimate about the two of them being here in the quiet kitchen in the dead of night sharing coffee. It seemed to make a mockery of all the arguments and heartache. This was what it would have been like if they had been able to resolve their differences. It made her suddenly determined not to give up. If there was a way of making Luis listen to her and finally accept what had happened in her past, then she knew with a sudden startling clarity that she owed it to them both to find it.

When he set the mugs down on the small table in the alcove and pulled out a chair, she went and sat down opposite him. She took a sip of the hot coffee, feeling it warming away the last of the chill. She glanced up at him. 'How does your shoulder feel now? Is that tablet starting to work?'

He nodded, sipping his own drink before replying, 'It seems to be easing a little.'

'I am sorry, Luis. I never meant to hurt you.'

'It is not always possible to avoid getting hurt.' He was speaking about something more than just the injury he had suffered, and she felt quick tears mist her eyes. She reached out and touched the back of his hand tentatively with the very tips of her fingers, afraid that even that small gesture would be misconstrued.

'I really am sorry, though, Luis...about everything.'

His hand remained where it was for an instant then slowly he drew it out from under hers, cradling his mug in both hands as he raised it to his lips although he didn't drink. 'Let us not rake over the past tonight of all nights, Laura. Neither of us is in any fit state to endure more arguments.'

'But there don't need to be any arguments,' she protested, then sighed wearily. 'I suppose you are right. We do seem to end up arguing every time we speak about it.'

'It is difficult to be impartial, but I have come to realise that it is something we must both try to be if we are to make this marriage work.'

'Do you really think it has a chance?' She laughed softly. 'I often think that you would have been so much better off if we had never met. You would probably have married Mercedes then.'

'It is pointless to speculate on things that can never be.'

'Perhaps but it is human nature to do so. Haven't you ever wondered what the future could have been like?'

'No. The present is all that is important to me.'

'I wish I could be like you then, Luis.' There were shadows in her grey eyes as she stared just past his head, lost in the dreams she'd once had. 'I used to build pictures of the life we would have before we married, imagining what it would be like living here with you, perhaps even having your children in years to come. Dreams, Luis, I know, but sometimes it is hard to destroy them even in the face of reality.'

She shifted her gaze to his face and was shocked to see the naked emotion there. 'Luis, I...'

He stood up, carrying the mug to the sink to rinse it awkwardly under the tap, his back rigid. He set it to drain on the worktop then turned. 'It is late, Laura. Time we were both in bed. I shall sleep in the room next to yours until my shoulder heals. That way I won't disturb you if I have to get up through the night.'

He was gone before she could find the words to call him back, but then what could she have said? To apologise for the agony she had witnessed so fleetingly on his face would have been crass beyond belief. Apologies would never compensate for all they had lost, her dreams and maybe at one time

Luis's also. All she could do was try to find a way to make him understand that she had never meant to trick him into this marriage. Maybe then there would be a chance to build fresh dreams for both of them.

It was over a week before the doctor allowed Luis to remove the bandages. By that time Laura knew that his patience had been tried to the limit. He was used to being active and the restriction in his lifestyle irked him. Not that it affected his work; in fact, he seemed to spend more and more time at the *bodega* only returning in time for dinner which in traditional Spanish style was served at ten each evening.

With her he was unfailingly polite, asking after her health, how she had spent her day, trotting out so many polite enquiries that she felt she would scream if she had to answer one more. Yet somehow she always managed to curb her temper and reply calmly, afraid to damage the fragile truce that had existed since that night they had shared coffee in the kitchen. She had the feeling that Luis was playing some sort of waiting game, a feeling heightened by the fact that he was still sleeping in the adjoining room. But waiting for what? That was the one question she couldn't answer.

It came as a shock, therefore, when she returned to the bedroom one morning after breakfast to find Luis standing by the window. He had usually left well before this time to go to work. Over the past week Laura had slipped into the routine of going down late for breakfast to avoid the intimacy of having to face him over the breakfast table. Doña

Elena nearly always took breakfast in her room, and Laura preferred the loneliness of eating by herself to the strain of having to cope with yet another polite conversation.

Now she halted in the doorway, her eyes widening as she saw that Luis wasn't dressed in one of his many elegant business suits but in tight black trousers and a short, waist-length dark grey jacket which made the most of his wide-shouldered, slim-hipped physique. With his black hair lying smoothly against his well-shaped head and his tanned skin gleaming with health and vitality, he looked superb, and she couldn't quite hide the faint hunger in her eyes as he suddenly turned to her.

He studied her in a silence that seemed to stretch for ever then smiled with a faint amusement. 'You seem surprised to see me. Surely you haven't forgotten what day it is?'

'What day? I'm sorry, I don't understand.'

'It is the beginning of the *feria*. Today we shall ride into town and meet our friends and enjoy all the celebrations at the fair. And I have brought you a present, something fitting for you to wear on such an occasion.' He gestured towards the bed and she gasped when she saw the dress lying on the white lace spread.

It was deep scarlet, the long skirt ruffled with layer upon layer of frills, the low-cut bodice and tiny cap sleeves edged with the same frills. It was a dream of a dress, exotic yet sophisticated, and she loved it on sight.

'It is just beautiful, Luis. Gorgeous! I don't know what to say. I heard your mother talking to you about the fair the other night at dinner but I never realised that we would be going or that you would give me anything as lovely as this to wear.'

'I am glad you like it, Laura.' His tone was warmer than she'd heard it for months, his dark eyes skimming her excited face. 'I decided to surprise you with it so I borrowed one of your dresses to have it made.'

'You had it made just for me? I don't know what to say!' On sudden impulse she went on tiptoe and kissed his hard cheek. His hands fastened around her waist to steady her then lingered for a heartbeat before he gently set her away from him.

'We shall need to leave in an hour or so. Can you be dressed and ready by then do you think?'

'Of course.' She went and picked up the dress and held it against her, trying not to feel just a tiny bit hurt by the way he had moved her away from him. He had gone to a lot of trouble to surprise her with this dress so surely that must mean that he cared something for her.

The thought brought a flush of happiness to her face and she smiled at him. 'Thank you, Luis,' she said softly.

'*De nada, querida*. Now I shall leave you to get ready.' He left the room and slowly Laura laid the dress back on the bed, her hand stroking down the soft ruffles. Perhaps she was being foolish to hope that this dress meant something but whatever reason Luis had for giving it to her, she was going to enjoy wearing it. She was going to put it on today and make herself look as beautiful as possible so that he would feel proud that she was his wife.

It fitted like a dream, the skirt clinging seductively to her slender hips before flaring gently over her thighs, the delicate ruffles swaying with every step she took. The bodice was far lower than she usually chose to wear but she had to admit that it looked good, making the most of her small firm breasts. Luis had even remembered to buy shoes to match it, slender-heeled red leather with thin straps which fastened across her ankle. Once she had slipped them on she stepped back to the mirror and studied her reflection, feeling a *frisson* of surprise when she saw herself.

She had drawn her blonde hair back into a heavy chignon at the back of her neck, anchoring it there with two thick tortoiseshell combs then on a sudden impulse had plucked a deep red rose from the display standing on the writing desk in the room and slipped it into one side of the silky knot of hair where it made a glorious contrast against her fairness. Over the past days she'd acquired a light tan so she'd used her make-up sparingly, just tinting her lips with a touch of scarlet lustre then darkening her lashes so that her grey eyes looked even more enormous and luminous than ever. She looked good, she knew, but what would Luis think when he saw her?

Butterflies were flitting around her stomach like crazy when she walked down the stairs. She took a deep breath then made her way to the salon, pausing uncertainly in the doorway but he must have heard her because he turned round. Just for a moment his face was unguarded, his black eyes glittering with a fierce possession as he skimmed her from head to toe, leaving her feeling shaken to the core by the emotion. Then he moved across the room, his tone bland as he took her hand and kissed her coolly on the cheek. 'You look very beautiful, *querida*. Don't you agree, Madre?'

Laura had been so caught up in Luis's reaction that she hadn't even noticed the older woman was in the room. She glanced across at her, surprised to find just the faintest hint of softness on Doña Elena's face as she studied her.

'I do. Luis is right, Laura. You look very beautiful in that dress.'

Flustered by the unexpected praise, Laura stammered out her thanks then jumped nervously when Luis took her arm. 'It is time that we were leaving. You are quite sure that you won't change your mind and come with us, Madre?'

'Thank you, but no. I don't feel up to all the excitement today. I prefer to stay at home.'

Luis nodded then led Laura from the room but instead of taking her towards the front door he steered her first of all into his study. 'I have something else for you, Laura.' He opened the drawer in his desk and took out a slim velvet case, unsnapping the lock to lift out a fragile strand of glittering gold which supported a delicate ruby pendant in the shape of a teardrop. It spun on the end of the chain, catching the light from the window so that it seemed to burn with a bright fire. 'I thought that this would be the perfect accessory to that gown.'

'It is beautiful, Luis, but I never expected such a present.'

'I cannot see why not. You are my wife, Laura. It is your right to have such things.'

'Is it?' She gave a shaky little laugh. 'I don't somehow think that I deserve a gift like this, Luis, not when our marriage is such a fragile thing.'

'We made a commitment to each other that cannot be broken. That is no fragile bond.' There was a hard, unbending note in his deep voice and she bit her lips as she averted her face, and heard him sigh roughly. He came around the desk, turning her so that he could fasten the chain around her neck, his hands steady as they dealt with the tiny clasp. When he had finished he turned her back, his fingers brushing her skin as he settled the ruby drop at the base of her throat.

'It is difficult for both of us, but let us agree to put aside our differences for this one day?'

She forced a smile, feeling the ache spreading. 'All right. I . . . I shall try, Luis.'

'Good.' He bent and brushed her cheek with a kiss that was too chaste and impersonal to be anything but a reward for her agreement, yet she felt her senses stir at once. When he offered her his arm, she slid her hand into the crook of his elbow, walking silently from the room and out of the front door. José was waiting on the drive for them, holding the reins of a showy grey horse. He smiled respectfully at them then said something to Luis as he handed him a flat crowned black hat. Luis put the hat on then turned to Laura, looking so elegantly right in the very Spanish outfit that her heart gave an unsteady little lurch then started to beat rapidly.

'You are not afraid of horses, I hope?'

'Well . . . no. Not really. Do you want me to ride into town?' She cast an uncertain glance at the huge grey, then glanced down at the ruffled scarlet dress.

Luis laughed, running a soothing hand down the animal's gleaming neck. 'Yes, but not quite the way you imagine.'

Laura frowned but before she could start to question what he meant, he mounted the horse then reached down and lifted her off the ground, settling her behind the saddle. She gasped, clutching at Luis's hard waist to steady herself as the horse shifted sideways before he calmed it with a few quiet words. He glanced over his shoulder at her, smiling broadly at her shocked expression.

'Do not worry, *querida*. El Duque is a gentleman. He will carry us both into town without missing a step, and this is the traditional way to arrive for the *feria*.'

Laura forced the nervousness down, smoothing the flowing skirt of her dress so that it lay against the animal's side in ripples of gleaming scarlet. When Luis urged the horse into a slow walk, she stiffened at once, her whole body tense until she found the rhythm.

'Slide your arm around my waist and that will make you feel safer.' Luis reached back and drew her right arm around him, holding her hand as they turned out of the gates and started towards the town. The action drew her closer to him so that her shoulder brushed against the hard muscles of his back under the sleek-fitting grey jacket, and a feeling which owed little to fear ran through her.

It took some time to complete the journey into Jerez at the slow pace Luis kept the horse to but

Laura didn't object. There was something magical about the swaying rhythm, the nearness of Luis's body to her own. She found herself leaning even closer to him and, when he gently laid her hand palm down on his muscular thigh and held it there, she felt as though her heart was going to beat itself right out of her chest.

The town was bustling with activity when they rode down the narrow streets. Everywhere there were couples riding just as she and Luis were, the women resplendent in their brilliantly coloured dresses, the men handsome in their elegant suits. There were whole families arriving in carriages pulled by horses decked out in garlands of flowers, the children bursting with excitement, their parents obviously proud of their offspring. Wherever she looked people were enjoying themselves, taking advantage of the glorious day. Laura had never seen anything like it, and said as much to Luis when he finally stopped outside the *bodega*.

'I thought you would enjoy it. Now it is time we joined up with some of our friends.' Looping an arm around her, he bent and let her slide to the ground then dismounted with a fluid ease. He caught her hands, holding her in front of him as he studied her face. 'You look like a child, *querida*, who has been given a treat.'

'Do I?' She couldn't help the sudden huskiness that softened her voice to little more than a whisper. Riding into town like that, so close to Luis, had heightened her senses to an almost unbearable degree so that just the touch of his hands on hers was making her feel feverish.

'*Sí*. A very beautiful and desirable child.' His voice had roughened, his hands tightening fractionally around hers. All around them there was talking, laughter, the sounds of people, yet suddenly it was as though they were the only two people left in the world. When she licked her parched lips his eyes darkened, his own mouth opening slightly as though to taste the feel of her tongue on his flesh. Laura could feel the heat of his body through the thin scarlet material of her dress, could feel it burning deeper and deeper inside her to warm a part of her that had been cold for far too long.

'But I am not a child, Luis,' she said softly, watching his face.

Colour swept in a fierce tide along his high cheekbones and he bent towards her. 'No, Laura, you are not a child but a woman...my wife.'

His mouth was gentle, yet the kiss burned. It melted the last of the ice, leaving her so achingly vulnerable that for a moment she felt afraid. Then suddenly she knew that it no longer mattered that she should try to fight him. She loved him and although he might never care, she wanted him to know.

She kissed him back with all the love she felt for him and felt his whole body jerk in reaction to the hot tide of emotion. Slowly he raised his head and stared down into her eyes then without a word led her inside the courtyard to where long tables had been laid with white cloths and heaped with food and wine. Several people stopped them but Laura scarcely heard a word they said, her whole attention focused on Luis and what had happened. There had been something different in his eyes just now. What it meant she had no idea. All she could do was hope that it promised well for their future, something to start to rebuild all those broken dreams upon.

It was a day which Laura knew she would always remember. It held a very special kind of magic that would claim part of her heart for ever. Now sitting under a tree as evening fell softly, she let her mind drift back over all the new sights she'd seen but the most special thing of all had been the way Luis had treated her. He had been warm and attentive all day long, letting her and everyone around them know in the clearest way possible that he was enjoying her company. Under such attention Laura had blossomed, even finding the courage to try out some of her shaky Spanish. The approval in Luis's dark eyes had been reward enough for that, and she smiled now as she remembered it.

'You are looking happy, *amada*. What are you thinking about?'

The deep voice stirred her senses to immediate life and she smiled up at him, uncaring that her heart must be in her eyes at that moment. 'You.'

'Is that so?' He dropped down beside her on the grass, taking off his hat to toss it aside and run his hand through his black hair. He glanced round at the throng of people then looked back at her with a faint lift of one dark brow. 'You have enjoyed today then, Laura?'

She felt a momentary disappointment that he hadn't pursued her answer more thoroughly but shrugged it aside at once. 'Of course. It has been a glorious day. And this has been a lovely ending to it.'

She looked round, smiling as she saw the way people were still chatting so animatedly after such a long day. The Spanish really knew how to enjoy themselves; most of the guests had spent the day at the *feria*, as she and Luis had done, then come straight on to Miguel Moreno's house for the barbecue.

'Miguel and his wife have worked hard to make the evening such a success. And it has been a success too for us, I think.'

It seemed an odd thing for him to say but before she could say anything another couple came up to speak to them. Laura joined in the conversation for a few minutes then got up and excused herself to go inside to the bathroom. There were several women already upstairs so she made her way to the bedroom which had been set aside for the female guests to repair their make-up.

Sitting down in front of the mirror, she smoothed a few stray wisps of hair back into the knot and refastened the combs to anchor it securely in place, then looked up with a smile when the door opened and another woman came in.

'Ahh, Laura, here you are? Not hiding, are you?' Mercedes walked into the room, the ruffled skirt of her elegant black dress swaying seductively as she moved. She walked over to the mirror and took a lipstick from her tiny black satin purse, touching it to her already perfectly made-up lips.

Laura took a deep breath, refusing to be drawn into the snappy reply that had been hovering on her lips. 'Of course not. I have no reason to hide.'

'In your position I doubt if I could be so sure. But I imagine that Luis is right to play things the way he has today.'

Mercedes slipped the lipstick back into her bag then ran a slender hand over her gleaming black hair, her eyes meeting Laura's in the mirror in a look of pure spite. Laura held herself rigid, fighting the demon in her head that was telling her to ask the woman what she meant by that statement but it was impossible to fight against it for long.

'What are you talking about?'

Mercedes shrugged, a faint smile curving her lips although her face was cold. 'Haven't you figured that out for yourself yet? Poor Laura, you really are blind. Why do you think Luis went to all this trouble today to bring you here and introduce you to all his friends? I imagine he even arranged for you to wear that dress.' She laughed at the betraying expression on Laura's face. 'Of course.'

'There is no "of course" about it...any of it! You don't know anything because Luis's reasons were quite simple and straightforward. He wanted to bring me because he enjoys my company the same as I enjoy his.' She shot the hot rebuttal back at Mercedes as she tried to push past her to leave the room. She didn't want to hear any more, didn't want the woman to spoil this day with her jealous, spiteful lies.

However, Mercedes' hand fastened around her arm, the long red nails like talons. 'I *know* because Luis confides in me. He tells me such a lot of things, Laura. You would be surprised to hear exactly what, I am sure. And he told me that he was intending to bring you today to quell all those unpleasant rumours about your marriage. It is amazing how easy it is to convince people that things are fine with just the right amount of acting, and he has done you both proud, all those tender little looks, the flattering attention. Yes, I am sure that most people will be convinced your marriage is as it should be, but I am not most people, Laura. I know the truth. I know that Luis regrets the day he ever met you!'

She let Laura's arm go and swept out of the room. Laura stared at the closed door, her heart around her feet. It was a lie, a cruel, vicious lie! Luis wouldn't have done such a thing. But even as she thought it another memory surfaced, the memory of his face that day when he had come to Rachel's house to get her, and suddenly she knew that she had to find out what the truth was.

The party had thinned out by the time she found Luis talking to a couple of men in the garden. She stood a little way away from them, her whole body trembling with the restraint she'd imposed on her emotions. She wouldn't break down now, she would hold on to her control while she found out the truth.

He must have seen her standing there because suddenly he was beside her. 'Is there anything wrong?'

'I don't know, Luis. Perhaps you can tell me the answer to that.' Her voice was stiff and she saw his face settle into taut lines. He drew her away from the group, his hand impersonal now at the small of her back.

'I suggest that you tell me what this is all about, Laura.'

How she hated that stiff note of authority in his voice! 'Yes, I think I should! Why did you bring me to the fair today? Was it just because you wanted to enjoy my company for a few hours or did you have another, far more sinister reason for doing so?'

'Such as?' He leant against a tree-trunk, relaxed and totally at ease. How she envied him that composure right then, because she felt as though any minute she was going to break into tiny pieces. Mercedes had been lying. She had!

'Come, Laura. You are obviously upset about something so let me hear it.' There was a thread of steel in his voice which cut her and she forced herself to carry on.

'Did you bring me here today so that it would look good and convince people that our marriage isn't in any kind of trouble?'

He gave her a long, cool look, his eyes so black that they gleamed like jet. 'What do you think Laura?'

The pain she felt was so raw that she staggered under the force of it. Just for a moment she stared at him with horror, unable to believe what she was hearing. There was a sudden slight movement to one side of where they were standing and she started nervously, her eyes suddenly meeting Mercedes's amused ones, and in that instant knew that it was true. This whole magical day had been a lie from start to finish!

With a tiny muffled cry, she turned and made her way across the garden, and if Luis even attempted to call her back she never heard him. She was deaf and blind to everything but the pain of realising that once more he had taken his revenge in the cruellest way possible.

At some point during this day she had started to rebuild her dreams, but now there was nothing left to build them upon any more.

CHAPTER SEVEN

THE days drifted past but Laura felt as though she was living in some sort of limbo. It was as though Luis's cruelty the day of the *feria* in tricking her like that had robbed her of something vital. She went through the motions of living but inside she felt hollow.

As to whether Luis understood how she felt she had no idea and didn't care. He was his usual polite self whenever they met over dinner but he made no attempt to cut through the barriers she had surrounded herself with. If Doña Elena noticed anything amiss she said nothing but occasionally Laura caught her watching her with a strange expression on her face. But it didn't matter what anyone thought. She could never forgive or forget the trick that Luis had played on her that day.

The only bright spot was that she received a letter from Rachel telling her that her brother Jack's business was taking off and that the desperate situation had eased. Laura was glad that her friend should be relieved of that terrible worry but she wasn't fool enough to believe that Rachel was completely in the clear. If she didn't continue to do exactly as Luis wanted then the situation could change in the blink of an eye. What a terrible trap for them all to be in!

It was a relief when Luis suddenly announced one evening over dinner that he would be away for several days. He had to accompany Miguel Moreno on a business trip to Amsterdam to finalise a new contract they were negotiating. Laura listened to him and his mother discussing the new contract without really hearing a word of what was being said. She picked up her spoon and pushed the sweet confection of whipped cream and cherries around but ate none of it. She hadn't felt like eating for a few days now, a feeling of nausea robbing her of her appetite, and it was beginning to show. When she had looked in the mirror tonight before coming down to dinner she had seen a new fragility to her slender frame. Perhaps it was possible for a person to fade away through lack of love.

Sudden hot tears sprang to her eyes and she set the spoon down knowing she couldn't stand this pretence a moment longer. Luis hated her and no amount of polite conversation would alter that one stark fact. With a muttered excuse she pushed her chair back and stood up, ignoring Luis's sharp enquiry as to whether she was all right. He could think what he liked, because frankly she no longer cared.

The house was quiet as she hurried from the dining-room and made her way outside to the small terrace. She stopped by the wall, gripping the stone balustrade with hands that trembled as she stared unseeingly across the vineyards. She had never felt so lonely and bereft in her life, not even when her father had died so tragically. They had been close after her mother had died and she had missed him dreadfully, but even that loss didn't seem so stark as what she was forced to contend with now. There was a gulf between her and Luis which could never be breached.

The tears streamed down her face silently. It was as though all the tension and heartache of months had suddenly caught up with her, reached a point where it had to break, and she cried as she hadn't done since she was a child.

'Here. Take this.' Luis was suddenly there, his voice quite impersonal as he offered her a spotless white handkerchief. Laura shook her head, rubbing the back of her hand across her wet face but the tears wouldn't stop and she heard him give a rough, impatient exclamation.

He caught her by the shoulder and swung her round, holding her in front of him as he wiped her wet face with a strangely gentle hand. Laura tried to shake him off, her eyes hating him as she glared up into his face. 'Let me go! I don't need your help, Luis. I don't need anything at all from you.'

'No? Is that so? Then why are you crying like this, as though your heart is ready to break at any moment?'

His voice was flat and without emotion; it seemed to set light to her temper and she dragged herself out of his hold and stepped back until she felt the hardness of stone against the back of her thighs. 'Is that why you imagine I am crying, for a broken heart?' She laughed harshly, snatching the handkerchief from him to wipe away the last of her tears. 'That would really boost your ego to think that, wouldn't it? It would give you such a feeling of satisfaction to know that your plan had been so successful!'

'You are upset, Laura. I think it would be better if you went upstairs.'

'Do you? How considerate of you, Luis. But then that is what you are, a very considerate man... on the surface.' She tossed her head so that the silky fall of pale hair slipped back over her shoulders. 'You don't really give a damn how I feel but you do like to keep up appearances, don't you? And what would the staff think if they saw me out here sobbing my heart out? They might start to imagine that there was something wrong and we can't have that, can we, Señor de Rivera? We can't spoil the image you are trying to project!'

'There is no point in discussing this while you are in such a state. I suggest you go inside and rest, Laura. I have noticed that you don't look your usual self recently.'

'Don't I? And I wonder why that might be? Could it possibly have anything to do with the fact that I am married to the biggest bast——'

'Enough! I will not tolerate any more of this hysterical behaviour. You forget yourself, Laura.' He caught her shoulders, his hands biting into her soft flesh as he gave her a tiny shake but it just seemed to incense her even more. She lashed out at him with her fists, all the pain and hurt she felt surging into one angry outburst of emotion.

Luis swore roughly, his voice harsh, his face set into angry lines that should have warned her but she no longer cared what he thought. 'I hate you, Luis,' she bit out. 'Hate you for the way you made me come here, hate you for what you tried to do to Rachel, hate you...'

'Because I won't fall under your spell the way I did once before!' All of a sudden his anger surfaced, his eyes blazing down into hers. 'I was a fool once, Laura, but I won't be one again. I know what you are now. I know how cleverly you used my desire for you to trick me.'

She wanted to hurt him, wanted to hit back at him as he had done to her. 'Yes, I did! You wanted me, Luis, but why should you have had me for free? Why shouldn't you have given me something in return...marriage?' She laughed in his face, the lies drawing her deeper and deeper into their horrible web as she saw his mounting fury.

'So at last the truth comes out. It is what I suspected all along, *querida*. It makes things simpler, you must agree?'

'I...what do you mean?' All at once the fight drained out of her and she stared at him in confusion, her heart lurching at what she saw in his eyes.

'I mean that there is no need for pretence any longer. We both know where we stand. You were willing to sell yourself to me for the price of a wedding-ring, and now it is left to me to enjoy what I have purchased with my money and name.' His eyes skimmed over her, lingering for a moment on her parted lips before dropping with deliberate appreciation to her high breasts.

'I...no! No, Luis. Look. I'm sorry but it was all lies. I was upset, angry, I just wanted to pay you back, but what I said just now wasn't really the truth!'

'I think it was the truth, and for the first time you actually admitted it. So why try to deny it all now?' He drew her closer to him, his hands sliding down her body, moulding her soft curves as he smiled into her white face.

'Don't. Please. Can't you understand that I was just trying to hit back at you?' She caught his wrist to stop his hand when it glided up to her breast but he merely captured both her hands in one of his and held them behind her back as he continued with the slow caress until she could feel her nipple throbbing under the skilful touch of his fingers. She closed her eyes, not wanting to see the triumph on his face as he felt her reaction, then gasped out loud when she felt herself being swung off her feet as Luis carried her down the steps from the terrace.

'Stop that! Put me down, Luis! Put me...' The words died instantly as he suddenly stopped and took her mouth in a kiss that held a very deliberate kind of passion. He knew her so well, knew how to make her respond to the pressure of his lips, the seductive sweetness of his tongue as it slipped between her parted lips. Laura gave a low, sharp moan of part protest, part desire as he forced her mouth wider open so that he could deepen the kiss to a level of intimacy that left her shuddering. It didn't seem to matter that she knew he was doing it deliberately, her response to him was instinctive. She had known little about the art of making love, despite what he believed, until he had taught her, and he knew exactly how to kiss her, how to let his tongue tease and arouse as he held her against his hard, warm body.

When he lifted his head she could barely open her passion-clouded eyes, but she forced herself to stare into his dark face. 'Don't do this, Luis. We...we shall both regret it. You must know that!'

He didn't answer her, his eyes hooded, yet she could feel the heat of his gaze against her as though he had touched her, and a slow throbbing ache started low in the pit of her stomach. When he started walking again she gave a sharp little cry of protest, pushing against the solid wall of his chest, but it was impossible to make him free her. His arms tightened around her, drawing her closer to him so that she could feel each heavy beat of his heart against her breast.

He carried her into the enclosed pool area and set her down on one of the padded loungers, sitting down beside her and trapping her there with his body as he bent over her. Laura gave a tiny gasping sob then tried to wriggle free, but he merely leant closer and smiled into her wide grey eyes.

'Why make such a fuss, *querida*? You know you want this the same as I do.' He stroked a hand down her from neck to thigh, the smile deepening when he felt the unmistakable hardness of her nipples pushing eagerly against his palm. Laura turned her head away in shame; he hated her and she knew it yet even that wasn't enough to stem the desire she felt to have him touch her.

'You like this, don't you, Laura?' His hand moved again, stroking, caressing, teasing her and she twisted helplessly.

'No! No, I don't like any of it!' The words were torn from her as she fought for control against the tormenting touch but they merely seemed to amuse him.

'No? Then I must find some other way to please you, *mi esposa*.' His voice was a low, vibrant thread in the dark night. It seemed to envelop her just as seductively as his hand now enclosing her breast, which stroked the nipple with the pad of his thumb until it peaked against the soft fabric of her dress.

Desire was a sharp, hot flame and despite herself she arched beneath his expert touch even as she gasped his name in a sobbing protest which he ignored as he turned his attention to her other breast and repeated the tormenting caress. Only then did he draw back, his voice steely as he caught her chin and made her look at him.

'You might be able to lie to me, Laura, but your body cannot. It shows me how much you enjoy my touch.'

She closed her eyes, knowing that what he said was true. Her mind might reject what he was doing to her, but her body ached for his touch. Even now she could feel surges of heat rippling deep inside her, and she shifted restlessly on the cushions, and heard him laugh softly just a moment before he took her mouth again.

The kiss was all and everything, fire and ice, fierce and tender, demanding and giving. Luis had never kissed her quite like this before and the shock of it drained all the fight from her so that she lay quiescent in his arms until his hands started to skim over her body in a tormenting dance which offered pleasure, hinted at desire yet stopped before she could savour the sensations. Laura writhed helplessly beneath the expert touch, her whole body throbbing with need. Luis would start a ripple then move his hands to start another, making her ache with frustration.

'Luis, please!' She caught his tormenting hands as she turned her head away to end the kiss, uncaring that he must surely hear the desperation in her voice. She couldn't take much more of this torment!

'So you admit that I can make you want me, do you, Laura? Admit that you can feel the desire inside you and the frustration of not being able to do anything to ease it?'

It was pointless to keep on denying something they both knew was true. 'Yes.'

'Then it is up to you to decide what you wish to do about it. Shall I stop now and let you go inside to your lonely bed? Or shall we both enjoy what we can give each other tonight?' His hand made a lightning-fast journey down her body, skimming breast and thigh, and she shuddered as she arched towards it. He was asking her to choose and the answer should have been straightforward; common sense should have overruled this hot desire which could only lead to yet more heartache, yet somehow it was difficult to make the choice.

Laura fought against the heady clamouring of her senses but it was a battle she was destined to lose when Luis moved slightly and she felt the hard pressure of him against her hip. He might be strong enough to play these games of passion to teach her a lesson, but he wasn't unmoved by them himself!

The thought was like balm. It soothed the shame she felt for her own weakness and changed all the rules in some indefinable way. Slowly she moved her hip, feeling the shudder which ran through him and smiled with a delicious amusement. Passion had always been on Luis's terms until now. He had instigated all their lovemaking but now she was going to show him something about his own needs, his own desires. Would he then be quite so confident of always being in control? She hoped not!

It took courage to slide herself upright on the lounger while he was watching her but she found it from somewhere. She reached out and ran her fingers down his broad chest, feeling the ripples of movement which instantly followed the light touch, as though every nerve in his body had sprung to attention. Just the realisation of that spurred her on so that it was suddenly easy to make the next move and feather a trail of kisses along the strong line of his jaw.

Luis sat like a statue, his whole body rigid, but there was no way he could prevent his heart from beating so betrayingly or her from feeling the heaviness of its rhythm under her hands as she smoothed them across his chest in a slow caress. He seemed to be barely breathing, his eyes so black that they glittered like glass as she drew back and looked at him but no one could call her breathing regular either. She had meant to teach him a lesson, to redeem herself by showing him that he too was vulnerable to desire, but now that seemed less important than the sensations surging to life between them.

For a moment they both stilled, dark eyes meeting grey in a silence which was so charged with tension that it felt as though the world was about to explode. Then Luis raised one brow in a silent challenge and Laura immediately responded to it.

She bent towards him and fitted her mouth to his in a kiss of such intensity that the air around them seemed to ignite. Luis groaned as he dragged her to him, his hands almost rough as they moulded her body against his while he murmured something to her in Spanish she couldn't understand and didn't need to as the fire between them burned out of control. Yet when he tried to ease her back against the cushions she resisted, filled with a sudden cold fear.

'Luis, I don't know if this is what I want!'

'*Dios*, Laura! What are you trying to do? Drive me insane?' His voice grated with strain, his mouth rimmed with white, evidence of the control he was exercising. Yet, even as Laura watched, that control snapped.

He stared down into her face, his eyes glittering. 'You have had long enough to make your mind up. Now I shall make the decision for you!'

The words were grated out just an instant before he took her mouth in a kiss which left no room for choice or even doubts. There was just her and Luis, and this raw desire they felt for each other. And for now that was more than enough.

Dawn came slowly, just a few fingers of light sliding through the dark sky at first. Laura lay in bed watching the rays spreading to tint the sky with rose and gold. Beside her Luis slept quietly, the sound of his steady breathing barely disturbing the silence in the room, yet it was the most precious sound she'd ever heard. It spoke of contentment and pleasure and a deep satisfaction, all of which she felt too.

She rolled over to look at him, letting her eyes enjoy the strong lines of his profile, the way the black hair fell in a heavy wave across his forehead. The urge to reach out and run her fingers through that silky hair was strong but she curbed it, knowing that it would be sure to wake him up, and just for now she wanted these few minutes to study him. She loved him so much that it hurt, but it wasn't like the pain she had lived with all these months. This pain was a hot, sweet feeling that seemed to fill her whole body, making her want to leap up and shout it from the window so that everyone could hear. She loved Luis de Rivera! That was something to shout about, especially after last night and what they had shared.

Laura closed her eyes, savouring again the intensity of their lovemaking both by the pool and here in this bed after they had come back inside the house. They had seemed to reach new heights together last night, as though barriers had been broken and souls had met. Surely it must mean that Luis cared for her, that it was more than just desire he felt for her body? She could only pray that it was so and wait until he woke to ask him.

She opened her eyes again, a faint smile touching her mouth as she turned to glance at him again then felt a shudder of sensation race through her when she saw that his eyes were open and that he was watching her. Just for a fleeting moment there was the fire of memory in his eyes then abruptly the flame was extinguished and replaced by a cool impersonality which chilled her.

When he tossed the clothes back and climbed out of bed, Laura watched without uttering a word because she couldn't think of what to say when she was so afraid of what the answer might be. Luis glanced round at her, arching a brow mockingly when he saw that she was watching him.

'I apologise if you were hoping for a repeat of last night's very enjoyable interlude but unfortunately work must come before pleasure. I have to be at the airport in just over an hour's time.'

Her face flamed at both the words and his tone but she forced herself to meet his gaze. 'I understand, Luis. Last night was...special, wasn't it?'

'It was very satisfying for both of us, proof that I was right.'

Did he have to sound so impersonal? It felt more as though he was giving their lovemaking a score: so many points for technique, so many for the level of passion! She sat up against the headboard, drawing the sheet over her breasts as she stared back at him. 'Right about what, Luis?'

'The fact that we can both still gain some pleasure from this relationship. It will be some compensation at least, don't you think?'

'I don't know what to think!' She pushed the tangled length of hair back from her face. 'You speak about compensation as though you feel you need something to make up for our marriage, but wasn't last night proof that we have something special going for us?'

'Last night we made love, Laura. We shared our bodies and found pleasure in doing so. I have never denied that I still desire you and there is no doubt that you feel the same. But if you are looking for something more from it then I am afraid you will not find it.' He slid his arms into a towelling robe he had left draped over the end of the bed after they had both showered last night. Laura's eyes dropped to the thick fluffy white fabric, remembering how it had felt when Luis had lifted her from the shower stall and wrapped her in the robe before carrying her back to the bed to continue making love. It had been just a few short hours ago yet now he slid the robe on and calmly dismissed the memories.

'Then nothing has changed? You still feel the...the same about me?' Her voice was quiet but he heard it because he turned to face her, and a shiver ran down her spine at the coldness of his expression.

'That is correct. A few pleasant hours spent making love cannot erase what you did, Laura. However, it does mean that we can enjoy a far more comfortable future together, which is some compensation.'

'Damn you, Luis! Damn you for your arrogance, your blindness, you cold-blooded self-righteousness! You won't even try to bend a little, will you? You have made up your mind and that is how things are. But if you imagine I shall ever repeat last night's mistakes then you are in for a shock!'

He walked calmly to the bed and sat down, ignoring the way she tried to shrink away from him as he slid a hand behind her head and drew her to him. With a galling ease he captured her mouth, his lips gentle yet insistent, wringing a response from her despite the anger and hurt she felt. When he had achieved what he had intended he let her go and stood up, smiling slightly as he studied her furious face and the trace of reluctant passion in her eyes.

'You will repeat last night and eagerly, Laura. Any time I choose. So please don't waste your breath telling me something we both know is yet another lie.'

He turned and walked into the bathroom, closing the door with a small final click that seemed to echo around the room. Laura snatched a pillow off the bed and threw it at the closed door then sank back as she realised the utter futility of the gesture. She could rant and rave, protest and threaten and nothing would change things. Luis knew that because he still held all the cards in his hands: Rachel and her father's welfare, even ultimately the success of Jack's business, and the final ace, the fact that she loved him.

How could she hope to beat a winning hand like that? And how could she face a future which was based on desire, not love? It might be enough for Luis, but she knew it would never be enough for her.

CHAPTER EIGHT

AFTER what had happened, Laura didn't expect to miss Luis, but she did. She missed seeing him at the dinner table, missed hearing his deep voice as he made some polite comment, missed just knowing that he was close by. She loved him so much despite everything that his absence was like a physical loss. How he would gloat if he knew that was how she felt! It would emphasise just how effective his plans for revenge had been.

The time seemed to drag as the days crept past and almost reached a week. Laura tried her best to fill in the hours but was hampered by a vague feeling of lethargy which seemed to make everything such an effort. Her appetite was still not what it should be, and on a couple of occasions she had to get up from the table with a murmured apology when just the sight of the food on her plate made her stomach churn. Perhaps she was sickening for something, she thought, but it was too much of an effort to even worry about that.

Luis's mother was quite uncharacteristically solicitous, begging her to rest, even suggesting that she should call her own doctor to visit Laura. But even though she appreciated this unexpected softening in the older woman's attitude towards her, Laura refused the offer. The only thing that was troubling her was this situation between her and

Luis, and no amount of pills and potions could cure that!

When Luis rang early on the morning he was due to fly home and coolly announced that he would be staying longer she found it impossible to hide her disappointment. Until that day, their conversations had been short and distant. It was expected that Luis would ring to speak to her and he carried out that duty religiously, each careful conversation a travesty of what it was supposed to be. Now, hearing the calm announcement, Laura couldn't help but snap back at him.

'I don't know why you even bothered to phone and tell me! What difference would it have made if I had objected, Luis?'

'None whatsoever. This is business and that must come before your childish outbursts.' His voice was suddenly icily cold and tears stung her eyes. She'd felt particularly rotten that morning when she had woken up, a bout of nausea sending her hurrying into the bathroom. Now the knowledge of how little he cared about her feelings tipped her emotions over the edge.

'It wouldn't have mattered what it was! Anything would come before me. Isn't that so?' she snapped back in fury.

There was a faint but noticeable pause before he replied and she went hot at the note that touched his deep voice. 'Are you missing *me*, *querida*? Or are you missing what I can make you feel?'

'I have no idea what you're talking about.' She twisted the curling lead of the phone around fingers that suddenly trembled.

'Oh, I think you have.' He laughed softly, a husky intimacy in the sound. 'I have missed you too, *mi esposa*, missed having you in my arms, missed the delights of your body. Is that what is wrong with you? Desire is such a potent addiction, *pequeña*. Once tasted it is almost impossible to do without.'

'I . . . no! Don't flatter yourself, Luis!' She recoiled as though he was there in front of her rather than at the other end of a phone connection.

'It isn't flattery. It is the truth, and I cannot see why you are so determined not to admit it. Does it not fit with that image you have in your mind?'

'What image? Look, Luis, if you——'

He continued as though she hadn't spoken, his deep voice silencing her. 'This image of being the poor rejected wife. You prefer to carry on making yourself believe that what you feel for me is love when in fact it is nothing half so complex, if such an emotion even exists, that is. You desire me, Laura, and you miss the satisfaction that I can give you. But do not fret, *amada*. Knowing how you are feeling, I shall do my best to return to you as soon as I can.'

He cut the connection and Laura put the receiver down as she tried her hardest not to cry. She could tell him that he was wrong, that she did love him, but he would never believe her because he didn't want to. He wanted to keep their relationship within the limits he had imposed upon it but she didn't think she could exist like that. When Luis came back then no matter what he threatened they would have to come to some sort of a decision about their future together, although she had no idea what it might be. All she knew was that living with him like this was destroying her.

That day seemed to drag even more than all the others. Doña Elena had an appointment in Seville and, although she offered Laura the chance to accompany her, Laura refused. She roamed around the huge house after the older woman had left, finding nothing there to occupy her despite the fact that the weather was gloriously hot and perfect for spending time in the pool. The enclosed pool area held too many disturbing memories for her to feel comfortable there while her emotions were so raw.

At a little before six she was sitting on the terrace sipping a glass of chilled lemonade when the sound of an engine broke through the silence. She set the glass down with a sharp clatter, her whole body tensing as she got up. Surely Luis hadn't managed to cut short his trip after all? However, when she walked around to the front of the house it wasn't Luis she found there but Domingo just climbing out of a racy red sports-car. He heard her approaching and turned to smile at her, his handsome face lighting up with that attractive smile that had won so many female hearts.

'Laura, *cómo estás*? Although I do not need to ask how you are when I can see for myself that you are as beautiful as ever.'

Laura laughed at the effusive compliment. There was something almost boyishly charming about Domingo's gallantry which was hard to resist. 'And I see that you have lost none of your "charm",' she pretended to scold him.

He leant a lean hip against the bonnet of the car as he pushed his sunglasses up on top of his head and grinned at her. 'A man has to try, especially in the presence of such a charming woman, and the woman he has come to beg to take pity on him.'

'The last thing I imagine you need is any woman's pity!' She walked the last few steps to stand in front of him, shading her eyes against the glare from the sun.

'Then that shows how wrong you can be to go by appearances. I am doomed to spend a lonely evening unless I can prevail upon your generous nature to have dinner with me.'

'I am quite sure that there are any amount of beautiful women who would bite your hand off to receive such an invitation, so why choose me, Domingo?'

'I enjoy your company, Laura.' He shrugged carelessly, a faint sadness in his face suddenly. 'And frankly just right now I am not interested in starting up a relationship with a woman. I have just—how do you say—yes, just had my fingers burned.'

'Oh, I see. Well, you do have my sympathies, Domingo,' she said softly. 'But I don't know if I can offer you a shoulder to cry on tonight.'

'Why not? I know Luis is still away. Mercedes mentioned it when she phoned earlier in the day to warn us that she would be changing her flight home.'

'Your sister is away somewhere?' Laura asked the question almost automatically as she pushed her hair back from her face. The sun was still hot despite the hour and she could feel perspiration beading on her forehead.

'Mmmm, in Amsterdam. I thought you knew because she has seen Luis while she's been there.'

The shock was so great that Laura felt all the blood drain from her face. Domingo must have noticed her reaction too because he stepped forward at once, but Laura put out a hand to fend him off. 'No, I'm fine. Just a touch too much sun, I believe.'

'Are you sure?'

'Yes, really.' She seemed to be functioning on two levels, one part of her reeling in pain from the shock of what she'd learned while the other somehow found the strength to make the polite dismissal of Domingo's concern. Was that the real reason why Luis had decided to stay away longer—because he wanted to spend more time with Mercedes?

'And I am just making matters worse by keeping you here.' Domingo slid the glasses down on to his nose with a smile of apology. 'I understand if you cannot accept my invitation of course, Laura. You probably don't feel like it if you have been out in the sun too long.' He started to swing himself back into the driving seat, obviously intending to leave, but suddenly Laura knew that was the last thing she wanted. Doña Elena was staying overnight with friends after she had attended to some business and tonight of all nights Laura didn't want to be by herself. She didn't think she could stand the thought of sitting in the huge empty house wondering what Luis was doing!

'I would love to come, Domingo. If you will just give me a few minutes to change?' She forced a smile and held it determinedly.

'You would? Wonderful! Take all the time you need, Laura. There is no need to rush.'

'Ten minutes,' she stated flatly, and turned to hurry inside the house. Somewhere deep inside, pain was tearing away at her, but she refused to bow down under its force now. Later she would have to deal with it of course...but not just yet. Not until she felt as if she was strong enough to cope.

The evening wasn't a success despite the fact that Domingo went out of his way to be a charming and attentive companion. He drove them up to Sanlúcar de Barrameda, a historic town just north of Jerez from where Columbus set off on his third trip to America and Magellan set off to sail around the world. With its golden sand beaches and beautiful old buildings, Laura knew she would have enjoyed seeing the town at any other time but not while she was fighting the demons in her mind.

She sipped a glass of the delectable sherry the town produced, called manzanilla, and pretended to listen to what Domingo was saying but that was what it was: pure pretence. If she had closed her eyes then she would have seen vivid evidence of what filled her mind, pictures of Luis and Mercedes together. She didn't think she could bear it!

She set the glass down, unaware that she spilled most of the wine on to the table, her eyes misted with tears. Domingo sighed, his face suddenly very grave. 'I think, Laura, that this has been a mistake. I have merely upset you rather than cheered myself up.'

There was something rather self-centred about his simple assumption, but Laura preferred that explanation to the truth. 'I'm sorry, Domingo. I have been poor company when you needed someone to listen to your troubles and offer a few words of advice.'

He sighed quietly, staring down at his empty glass. 'The thing I need most, Laura, is to face up to how I feel, and that scares me. Admitting you love someone is a terrifying thing to do. There is always the chance that you will have your love rejected.'

Didn't she know that? Only too well, in fact. With a murmured excuse she pushed her chair back while Domingo signalled to the waiter for the bill. Hurrying into the ladies' rest-room, she ran water into the bowl and washed her hands, giving herself time to collect herself again. She was silly to take Domingo's wry words to heart so much. It was just that her nerves were so raw at present and it didn't help that she was beginning to feel nauseous again although she'd taken care to avoid any overly spicy dishes on the extensive menu. The bouts of sickness were starting to become a nuisance; only that morning she'd had to rush to the bathroom as soon as she'd got up...

She stared at her reflection in the mirror above the basin, her grey eyes wide with shock. How could she have been so stupid? The signs had all been there but she'd been so caught up in the misery of her situation that she'd overlooked them. She dried her hands on a towel then opened her bag and searched through it with hands that shook until she found her diary and started checking dates then sat down abruptly on the velvet-covered chair and closed her eyes.

She was pregnant. It was the only thing that made sense and could explain the lethargy, the nausea and increasing bouts of sickness. How could she have been so dim-witted as not to realise it sooner? But what was going to happen now? Would this bring her and Luis closer, or would it drive them even further apart? Would he want the child, when he hated her so much?

Tears welled up in her eyes but she blinked them away. She couldn't start to think that way now. She had to hold on to her composure until she was safely back in the Casa de Flores, then she would think it all through and decide which way she was going to approach Luis with the news.

She got up to go then paused as she caught sight of herself in the mirror. One hand slid to her stomach and pressed lightly against its flatness as though by touching it she could feel the child growing there. No matter what happened between her and Luis she wanted this child and would love it. It was a part of him which would always belong to her.

It was almost one a.m. before Laura stepped from the taxi in the driveway. She said goodnight to the driver then walked wearily towards the house with a heavy sigh. It must have been Fate that had dictated that Domingo's racy red car should break down tonight. It had taken them hours to find a garage willing to send out a mechanic to the vehicle but even then it couldn't be mended. A new radiator would have to be ordered from England before the car would be back on the road. Laura had left Domingo still arguing forcibly with the mechanic, ignoring his protests that he would accompany her if she would wait, to get into the taxi

she'd managed to summon. She only wished that
she'd had the foresight to call it a couple of hours
earlier, then she wouldn't be getting in so late.

She climbed up the shallow steps to the front door
and felt in her bag for the key, then jumped when
the door was suddenly swung open.

'Where in the name of all the saints have you
been?'

She was so surprised to see Luis standing there
that she stared at him without uttering a word and
heard him curse roughly. He caught her under the
elbow and half lifted, half dragged her inside,
towering over her. 'I asked you where you have been
until this hour. Now answer me, Laura!'

His voice was so hard that it seemed to cut deep
into her and she flinched away from him instinc-
tively. 'I . . . out to dinner.'

'By yourself? Or were you with someone?' He
laughed deeply, bending so that he could stare in-
solently into her face. 'You don't need to answer
that question, Laura. Obviously you were with
someone. Who?'

She took a deep breath, fighting to remain calm
in the face of his hostility. 'Domingo asked me to
have——'

'Domingo? You were with him? Have you no
shame at all, Laura? Or did you do it deliberately
to shame *me*?' His fingers were suddenly hard
around her wrist, his face dark with anger. Laura
pulled against his hold, glaring up at him although
she could feel the pain of the accusation right
through her.

'I had *dinner* with Domingo. Is that a crime, Luis?'

He ignored her question in a way that fuelled her temper, his arrogance over-riding it. 'Dinner? It must have been a very long meal. Or did dinner stretch to something more? Is that why you are so late, *querida*?'

She refused to rise despite her growing anger, refused to dignify the suggestion by repudiating it. 'Domingo asked me to have dinner with him and drove us to Sanlúcar. Unfortunately, his car broke down on the way back and that is the reason why I am so late. Now if you will excuse me, Luis, I am very tired.' She walked past him but got no further than a couple of steps before he spoke.

'And how did you pass the time until help arrived?' His eyes skimmed her with icy contempt, his cheekbones edged with a thin line of red that hinted at the fury he was controlling. 'Was it a long and boring wait, or did you and Domingo find some *pleasant* way to fill the hours?'

A cold hand gripped her heart but she faced him proudly. 'I won't even dignify that with an answer, Luis.'

'Why not? Because you are afraid that I would know that you were lying by your voice? Why did you accept Domingo's invitation, *mi esposa*? For the promised dinner or because you had other...appetites which needed feeding?'

She wasn't aware of taking those few steps back towards him, wasn't aware of raising her hand. It was only when she felt the stinging of her palm as flesh struck flesh that she realised what she had done. For a moment she stared at the white patch on his lean cheek, watched while it slowly turned red, then spun on her heel and ran up the stairs with a sob. She fled into the bedroom and threw herself face down on the bed then rolled over with a sharp gasp of alarm as the door bounced open with a force that set it straining against its hinges.

'You take me for a fool, Laura, or try to. And that is a dangerous mistake. I understood how you were feeling this morning and that is why I changed my plans and came home tonight, but obviously I could have saved myself the trouble. Your... needs had already been satisfied.

She felt ill at the contemptuous mockery in his voice. Did he really believe that she and Domingo had... She couldn't bring herself to even think it, let alone do it! Yet as she sat up and swung her feet off the bed she could see the truth on Luis's face and the pain and anger swamped her.

'And what about your needs, Luis? Have they been satisfied? How convenient it must have been for you to discover Mercedes was in Amsterdam also. Or was it just a fortunate coincidence? Perhaps you and she arranged it. After all, you said yourself that once a person has tasted desire it becomes an addiction.'

His face was like thunder, his body stiff with suppressed rage as he slowly closed the door and came towards the bed. 'You have the nerve to say that, to try to assuage your guilt by accusing me?'

She shrugged with a forced indifference. 'If the cap fits, as the saying goes. Maybe you have something similar in your own language, darling.'

Her legs were trembling when she stood up but she walked over to the mirror and started to pull the pins out of her hair, letting it slide around her shoulders. She picked up the brush then held it in her hands as she looked at Luis through the mirror. 'I don't think there is anything else to say.'

He smiled but it was a mere travesty of amusement. 'Don't you? Mercedes was in Amsterdam on business for her father. I do not intend to allow you to sully her reputation to save your own.'

'Of course not! Nothing must ever be said about pure sweet Mercedes! Aren't you sorry that *she* isn't your wife, Luis?'

'I have regretted our marriage many times, Laura, but never more so than tonight!' His voice was flat, his face so cold that she could hardly bear to look at it. He turned to walk from the room but suddenly Laura knew she couldn't leave things like this. Anger and hurt were two emotions that had blighted their relationship for so long now—too long, in fact. She had to think about the child she was carrying. She couldn't bring it into the world to live with parents who could barely speak to one another.

'Luis, please listen to me. I...Domingo and I just went for dinner. There was nothing more than that to the evening. He was upset over a relationship which had broken up and when he...' She swallowed down the bile of the words. 'When he found out from his sister that you were staying on in Amsterdam he called round to see if I would lend him a shoulder to cry on. The car broke down,

that is why I am late, but nothing...
nothing...happened between us!'

He glanced back at her, one dark brow raised in
arrogant disbelief. 'And you really expect me to believe that?'

'Yes!' She controlled the urge to shout back at
him and spoke quietly. 'You have no reason not to
believe me, Luis, and you know that. But if you
have any doubts then phone Domingo and let him
verify my story.'

'And give him the satisfaction of realising that I
am willing to go crawling to him just to hear that
my wife has kept her marriage vows! I think not,
Laura.'

'But it is the way to rid yourself of all these stupid
doubts! Why won't you just accept that I am telling
you the truth, Luis?'

His hand gripped the edge of the door, turning
white from the pressure he was exerting. When he
looked at her, Laura could see the anger lying rawly
in his eyes. 'Because I will never, ever believe
another thing you tell me after the way you misled
me before our marriage.'

'I made a mistake, Luis! Am I to be punished
for the rest of my life because of it?'

'If that is what it takes, yes! But do not think
that I shall overlook any further "mistakes", *mi
esposa*. If this evening's jaunt with Domingo was
a taste of what you are planning for the future then
you would be well advised to think again. You are
my wife and you will remain my wife. There will
be no liaisons, no pleasant little dalliances with

other men. I shall not countenance such actions!'

'But it will be all right if you have your liaisons, your dalliances? Is that right, Luis? There will be one rule for you and one for me?' She laughed with a faint hysteria then bit her lip to control it. 'What a hypocrite you are, Luis! It doesn't matter what you and Mercedes get up to as long as I know my place!'

He was beside her in a trice, his hands gripping her shoulders as he half lifted her off her feet and glared with fury into her face. 'I have heard enough, more than enough! You are in danger of pushing me too far, Laura, and you wouldn't like the consequences.'

'I don't like what has happened so far, so how could things turn out worse than this?' A sob escaped from her lips but she held the others back from following it as she stared at him with tear-soaked eyes. 'This is no life, Luis. Not for you or me or... or the b...'

'This is all there is. Never doubt that! And it is more than you can expect if there is any repeat of tonight.' He removed his hands from her shoulders as though he found the feel of her somehow repugnant. 'If I ever learn that you have done such a thing again with Domingo or anyone else then you will quickly regret it, Laura. I will not allow you to make a fool of me!'

He strode from the room and after a few seconds Laura heard the sound of a car door slamming and an engine roaring as he shot down the drive. She walked slowly to the window to watch the gleam of its tail-lights until they disappeared into the night and the distance between her and Luis had never seemed more insurmountable.

This should have been one of the happiest nights of their lives, the discovery that they were going to have a child. But until she was sure how Luis felt about the idea then she couldn't tell him. She didn't think she could bear to hear him say that he didn't want their child because of his hatred for her.

CHAPTER NINE

WHERE had Luis been all night?

The question drummed inside her head as Laura stepped down into the hall. It was barely seven in the morning but she'd been unable to stay in the room any longer. After Luis had left she had undressed and got into bed then lain awake hour after hour listening for the sound of him returning, but to no avail. By the time she finally fell asleep just as dawn was breaking he still hadn't returned and her heart was heavy with worry in case something had happened to him. He had been in such a temper when he'd driven off. It would have been only to easy for him to have...

The thought died in an instant, relief like a warm tide when she walked out on to the terrace and saw him standing staring out towards the fields. He was still wearing the same clothes he'd worn last night, the beige suit creased now, the toning cream shirt less than crisp. His dark hair was windblown across his forehead, his jaw darkly shadowed with beard, but to Laura's eyes he looked just marvellous. She stepped forward, relief making her eyes glow with warmth as she traced his muscular figure to reassure herself that he was all right.

'Where have you been? I was worried about you.' Her hand lightly touched his arm, the gesture quite spontaneous and unconsidered.

He glanced down at her hand then deliberately moved away so that it fell from his arm. 'How touching. However, where I have been is my business not yours. I am not accountable to you for my whereabouts, Laura.'

She couldn't bear it! Couldn't bear this constant hostility, the harsh words that told her how little he cared when she loved him so much. With a tiny whimper of distress she pushed past him and hurried down the steps but she'd got no more than a few yards when Luis caught her arm and stopped her. 'Laura, I...'

'What? Want to show me again how little you care that I was worried about you? Don't bother, Luis. You've made your contempt for me and my feelings more than plain.'

She pulled against his restraining hold but although he didn't hold her arm tightly, he refused to let her go. He sighed roughly, 'Sometimes I cannot believe that I am saying these things to you, Laura. I never imagined that one day what we once had could turn to this.'

'Neither did I, Luis.' She laughed shakily, more affected by what he had said than she knew was wise. 'I loved you so much when we married. I thought that I had suddenly reached out and been given a slice of heaven but it couldn't last, could it. It was too wonderful for that.'

He stiffened at her words, his hand falling from her arm as he turned away. Laura's heart ached at the mixture of emotions she saw in his face. She was hurting, but was he also? Yet he would never admit it to her or even to himself. That damnable pride of his was too strong to ever let him do such a thing.

The realisation made her linger when common sense told her to go. Surely it was worth one last attempt to try to bridge this gap between them? There was the baby to think about, after all—their child. That could be the bond that would heal the rift if only she could start the healing process by making Luis listen to what she had to tell him.

'I never meant to deceive you, Luis. I've told you that so many times but you have never believed me. No!' She was the one who stopped him when he uttered a rough curse and turned away. 'Every time I try to explain you walk off and it's not fair to either of us! You have cast me as some sort of scarlet woman and that's not true.' Her fingers fastened tighter around his arm as she stepped directly in front of him to block his path.

'I do not wish to discuss this. You know my views.'

'*You* do not wish to discuss it? This isn't the Dark Ages, Luis. You aren't the lord and master no matter that half the people in this town treat you that way!' Her eyes were stormy, her face flushed as she glared into his set face. 'I was eighteen years old and in my first year at university. My father had just remarried and moved to Australia. He...he was killed there a few months later in a road accident and it felt as though the bottom had fallen out of my world. I'd never felt so lonely in the whole of my life.'

'Enough! I do not want to hear this, Laura.' His voice was hard, his eyes glacial but suddenly she didn't care any longer. Whatever happened now couldn't be any worse than what had happened so far.

'Well, I'm afraid this time you are going to hear it.' When he made a move to step around her she sidestepped and made him stop again. 'If you don't want to stand here and listen then I shall follow you into the house and if one of the servants overhears my sordid little tale then you only have yourself to blame!'

She was shaking so hard that she thought she was going to collapse but she forced herself to stand in front of him and ignore the burning anger in his eyes that would have made many a man think twice or three times about a course of action. But she was fighting not only for her own future but that of her child as well, and that gave her the strength. 'I met Martin at the university. He was in his final year, reading psychology. He was warm, friendly and full of fun. We started going out together and it wasn't long before I convinced myself I was in love with him.' She gave a light, brittle laugh. 'I needed someone so much just then that it wasn't difficult. We...we slept together just once, that's all, Luis.'

'*Dios*! Do you imagine that I want to hear this? Do you?' All of a sudden he was holding her, his fingers bruising as they bit into her flesh. Laura strove for calm knowing that the last thing she must do was allow this to deteriorate into yet another argument.

'No, I'm sure you don't. I don't want to tell it to you, Luis, but it has to be told. You have to understand!' She swallowed down the pain, keeping her voice calm as though by that way she could soothe him into listening to her tale. 'I thought...imagined that sleeping with Martin signalled some kind of commitment between us but I was so wrong it was laughable almost. After that night he didn't ring or call around to see me for almost a week and every time I tried to contact him he was unavailable. Finally, I ended up waiting outside the lecture hall for him one day.' She gave a faint smile, her eyes clouded as the memories of that painful time returned. 'He wasn't pleased to see me. That's an understatement. If he could have avoided me he would have done but I refused to be fobbed off any longer. I made him tell me what was wrong, why he hadn't phoned or tried to see me and in the end he admitted what his reasons were. He didn't want to get too involved with anyone, he said. If he had known that I...that I had been a virgin before that night we spent together then he would never have allowed it to happen.'

She tossed her hair back as the breeze blew it across her cheek, unaware now of the biting grip of Luis's hands upon her. 'It was almost funny really; there was I imagining that night was proof of how much he loved me and the commitment we were making to one another, while to poor Martin it had all turned out to be some awful nightmare. After that, well, I swore that I would never allow anything like that to ever happen again. I had learned my lesson and it was a bitterly painful one, Luis. One I could never forget.'

She looked up at him, studying the hard implacable lines of his handsome face while she prayed that this time he would understand. 'There were

never other men, Luis. Just that one unhappy
mistake.'

There was silence for a moment and she held her
breath. Then slowly Luis let his hands fall to his
sides and walked around her.

'Luis!' There was an ache in her voice, a plea for
him to stop, but he carried on walking. Laura
clenched her hands, her whole body rigid. 'Doesn't
what I have told you make any difference?'

He stopped then and glanced back, his face
blank. 'It might have done if you had told me before
we married. Now it is of little consequence.' He
smiled coldly. 'You cannot imagine how worried I
was about our wedding-night. I was so afraid of
hurting you, *querida*, because I believed that you
were a virgin. Then, at first, when you seemed to
overcome the discomfort and find pleasure in our
loving I was so proud. My lovemaking was giving
you joy and fulfilment! But then suddenly I realised
how mistaken I was; you weren't untouched and
innocent at all. It had all been a pretence. You
weren't a virgin but merely pretending to be one.'

'No! It wasn't like that, Luis! I had . . . had made
love just that one time and years before. There was
discomfort but I forgot about it because your loving
was everything I could have dreamed it would be.
But it wasn't an act. I loved you! Surely the fact
that I told you the truth proves that?'

'All it proves is that you have a noisy conscience.' He laughed with bitter contempt. 'You
couldn't live with the lies any longer, and why
should you do so? We were married then; you had
achieved what you had set out to. You just expected me to listen to your tale then forgive and

forget what you had done, but that is something I shall never do!'

He carried on up the steps to the terrace but this time Laura made no attempt to stop him. There was no point, when nothing would change his opinion of her.

She had no idea how long she stood there, her head full of the bitter scene that had followed her confession. She had never anticipated that his anger would change to hatred as it had done. Yet was it really any wonder? What she had done must seem to him to have been totally premeditated. She had hurt him, yet there was no way that she could make up for it when he was determined to keep her at bay. She had done it all out of love yet that didn't make it any better. The fact that Luis might have understood if she had told him the truth before their marriage was the cross she would always have to bear.

It was only when she heard the sound of Luis's car going down the drive that she finally roused herself. She went back to the terrace, forcing a smile when she found Pilar there laying the table. The girl jumped nervously when Laura suddenly appeared.

'Oh, excuse me, *señora*. I did not know that you were up yet. Shall I tell Cook that you are ready for breakfast?'

Laura shook her head. 'No, thank you, Pilar. I don't really feel like anything just yet.'

'You should try to eat something, *señora*.' The maid smiled shyly, her gaze dropping meaningfully to Laura's stomach before returning to her face. 'It will help the sickness.'

Laura felt her face fill with colour and she looked away, murmuring that she would have coffee and toast, then. When Pilar had hurried back inside she sat down at the table and closed her eyes with a sigh. Obviously others had put two and two together and come up with an answer to explain her recent bouts of nausea faster than she had herself! Did that include Doña Elena? Could Luis's mother's solicitous attitude of late be attributed to that same guesswork? If so, then it wouldn't be long before Luis was made aware of everyone's suspicions. She could only imagine what he would think if he found out about the baby from somebody else! The last thing she needed right now was for relations between them to deteriorate any further.

Pilar came back with the toast and coffee, smiling her approval as she laid them out on the table. Laura poured herself a cup of the fragrant coffee then sipped it slowly while she tried to work out what she should do. The thought of telling Luis that she was pregnant scared her when she wasn't sure what his reaction might be, but there was no way she was going to be able to put it off much longer.

She buttered a triangle of toast then took a small bite and forced herself to chew it slowly as she felt her stomach revolt at the taste. She smiled with bitter wryness, realising that she wasn't going to have a choice much longer. Luis was far too sharp not to notice that something was wrong if she started leaping up from the table all the time! She would make an appointment to see the doctor this morning, then if her, and everyone else's, suspicions proved to be correct would decide when and how to tell Luis the news. After that...well, only time would tell what happened next. The one real consolation was that, no matter what, she would have Luis's child to love.

She was pregnant.

Laura left the doctor's office in a daze, still hardly able to take it in. It was one thing suspecting that she might be and quite another having it confirmed as indisputable fact.

Without really being aware of where she was going, she walked along the street towards the centre of the town, barely conscious of the people milling all around her. Her head was full of the child she would have in a few months' time so that it was several seconds before she realised that someone was calling her name.

She glanced along the street and felt some of her joy evaporate when she recognised Mercedes, elegant as ever in a slim-fitting burgundy two-piece. When the older woman started to cross the road, Laura steeled herself, but it was impossible to quell the animosity that rose inside her.

'Ahh, Laura, what a surprise to see you in town. Are you doing some shopping?' Mercedes glanced at the small bag Laura was carrying with a coolly polite smile which did little to hide her dislike.

Laura responded with an equally chilling politeness whilst inside she felt anger starting to burn at the thought of the time Mercedes and Luis had just spent together. 'I had an appointment. Now I am on my way to see Luis.'

'Then how fortunate it is that I met you. I can save you making a wasted journey.' Mercedes smiled, her eyes filled with triumph as she saw the angry flush creeping up Laura's face. 'Luis mentioned on the flight home that he had an appointment which will take him out of town this afternoon. I am surprised that he didn't mention it to you, but then I don't think that he discusses business with you all that often.' She laughed huskily. 'You *did* know that Luis and I were in Amsterdam together, Laura?'

'Of course. Naturally Luis told me.' If it took every ounce of strength she possessed she would hold on to her composure and not give the woman the satisfaction of knowing how much it had hurt to discover that fact. 'You were there on business for your father, I believe.'

'Mmmm, but it is often possible to combine business with pleasure, isn't it? And Luis and I always enjoy one another's company whether it is in a business capacity or... any other.'

She couldn't take much more of this, couldn't stand there and listen to all these half-veiled insinuations which were breaking her heart. 'I am sure you do. However, if you will excuse me, I think I shall see if I can catch Luis before he leaves.'

'Don't you believe me, Laura? I can assure you that I am telling you the truth about the appointment.' Mercedes laughed again, making no attempt to hide her amusement. 'Luis often acquaints me of his whereabouts in case I ever need to contact him for any reason.'

Laura's blood was starting to boil, heated by all the pain and anger she could feel inside her. 'Luis is my husband. Perhaps you should try acquainting yourself with that fact!'

Mercedes shrugged lightly, not at all perturbed. 'It makes little difference to Luis so why should it worry me? Besides, once Luis's plans have reached fruition then your role will be over and done with.'

'What do you mean? What plans?' Suddenly all the anger drained out of her, leaving her feeling oddly shaky. Laura reached out a trembling hand to steady herself, feeling the warm roughness of the brick under her icy fingers.

Mercedes studied her in silence then gave a defiant toss of her head. 'Why shouldn't you know? Maybe then you will start to understand the hopelessness of your position. Do you imagine that Luis is in love with you, Laura, and that is why he is making such a determined effort to hold your marriage together?' She laughed when she saw the shock on Laura's face. 'You see, I know so much more than you imagine, don't I? Perhaps by realising that you will believe that what I am telling you is the truth.'

'And what is this truth, Mercedes? What are these...these plans that Luis has?' Her voice barely carried above the sounds of the traffic but the older woman heard her clearly it seemed because she answered at once.

'A child. An heir for the Rivera family business. That is why Luis is holding this marriage together. Divorce is not possible in our religion. You understand that. And Luis needs an heir, a *legitimate* heir, to carry on the family name; a child you will give him, Laura. After that—well...' She shrugged meaningfully. 'After that, your role in Luis's life will be over. Naturally you will be well compensated but at least it will mean that he will be spared living this way.'

'No! I don't believe you. It's barbaric!' Laura recoiled against the wall, her face ashen, her whole body trembling as though she had a fever yet she felt so cold that she was almost numb.

'It is your choice to believe me or not, but it is the truth, Laura, as you will find out for yourself if you stay. Frankly, I don't really care. It will not affect the relationship I have with Luis.' She went to walk away but Laura caught her arm.

'You are lying, Mercedes! You are!'

'Am I? Think about it. Add it all up, everything that has happened, and then decide if I am lying or not.'

'I shall go to Luis and ask him. Make him tell me the truth and then if it is all lies think how angry he will be with you!' There was desperation in her voice but Mercedes merely smiled as she drew her arm away from Laura's hold.

'Do you think that would be wise...after last night? Luis might suddenly decide that even getting the heir he wants so desperately isn't worth all the trouble you cause him, Laura. And where will that leave you? At least by going along with his plans you are assured of always being looked after, always having more than enough money to live on. Now, if you'll excuse me, I...'

'Did Luis come to you last night after...after we quarrelled?' She didn't want to ask that question, wanted even less to hear the answer, but it had to be said and heard. How else could Mercedes know about what had happened?

Something flickered in Mercedes' eyes before her lids lowered. 'Do I need to answer that?'

She walked away but Laura made no attempt to stop her this time. That last cool statement seemed like the final betrayal, proof of how little Luis cared for her. He had left the house and gone to Mercedes, spent the night in her arms, telling her of his plans for the future, plans that held no place in them for Laura. It seemed incredible that any person could be so cold-blooded and ruthless, but the more she thought about it the more it explained about Luis's behaviour towards her. He had brought her back to Spain and to his house, made love to her for that one reason: a child that would carry his name.

A sob welled from her lips and she pressed a hand to her mouth as she felt the hot, bitter tears gathering in her eyes. What a fool she had been, a stupid, blind fool not to have realised just how deep his desire for revenge ran. And what greater revenge could he have than taking her child away?

She had run away once before but always hoped that he would find her. Now she had to run again, only this time she had to make certain that she disappeared without a trace. She loved him, but she would never let him take something so precious away from her!

It seemed to take forever to get back to the house and throw a few things into a bag. She wouldn't have bothered returning in truth if it hadn't been for the fact that she needed her passport. Now as she searched desperately through the drawers, she moaned softly in distress as she failed to find it.

Where was it? It was difficult to remember the last
time she had seen it but she forced herself to stand
quite still and try and felt a surge of relief run
through her when she suddenly recalled Luis men-
tioning something about putting it away in the desk
with his.

Leaving the small overnight bag by the bed, she
ran down the stairs and into the study, her hands
shaking as she pulled open the drawers until she
found the missing passport in the very bottom one.
She snatched it up then half turned to leave the
room, stopping abruptly when a familiar voice said
softly, 'Did you want something, Laura?'

Her heart jolted painfully, her breath catching as
she glanced over her shoulder to where Luis stood
in the doorway watching her. How much had he
seen of her frantic search? Had he seen her take
the passport from the drawer? She swallowed down
the sudden wave of sickness as she slid the small
book into the pocket of her skirt and turned to face
him. 'I...I was just looking for an envelope,' she
lied. 'I wanted to write to Rachel and suddenly
found that I had run out but it doesn't matter. I
can get some the next time I'm in town.'

She sidled around the desk, freezing when Luis
moved further into the room, one dark brow raising
fractionally as he studied her pale face, the feverish
glitter in her eyes. 'You seem upset, far more upset
than the discovery that you had run out of envelopes should merit. Are you sure there isn't
something else wrong?'

'No! Well, yes. I mean I do feel a bit sick if you
really want to know.' She bit her lip, suddenly
wishing that she hadn't used that as an excuse of

all reasons, but Luis mercifully seemed unaware of any undertones as he moved closer to her and studied her with open concern.

'When did it start? Do you think you have some sort of virus, Laura? Do you want me to call the doctor to see you?'

Such concern hurt, especially following hard on the heels of what she had learned that morning and she backed away from him with contempt in her eyes. 'What a hypocrite you are, Luis! As if you really care one way or the other if I am ill.'

His face closed, his eyes glittering dangerously. 'Naturally I care how you feel, Laura.'

'Why? In case my being sick hinders your rotten plans?'

The words flowed out before she could stop them, the memories of all Mercedes had told her so rawly painful that they drove away any thoughts of caution just for a moment. But one thing she couldn't afford to forget was how astute Luis was. If he suspected that she knew what he had planned on doing then it wouldn't take him long to realise just how she would react. The last thing she needed was him watching over her right now!

'What plans, *querida*? Why do I get the feeling that you are keeping something from me?' He stepped closer, tilting her chin with his finger as he studied her face with an intensity that made her squirm. It felt as though he was looking right into her soul, laying all her secrets bare, but there was one secret she had to hide from him! If he found out about the baby then she would never get away!

She closed her eyes as she took a slow breath and fought for calm then opened them slowly to look

back at him as steadily as she could. 'You are imagining things, Luis. Perhaps I am a bit over-
wrought but that is understandable after last night
and... and this morning.'

He sighed deeply, letting her go as he turned to
the window and stared out across the terrace. 'You
could be right. I too am feeling the strain of living
the way we do. Sometimes I wish that we could
turn back the clock and start all over again.'

'You do?' Unconsciously her voice softened. She
took a slow step towards him, her whole body rigid
with tension. 'Then why can't we, Luis? Why can't
we do just that, forget all these dreadful months
and just remember how we once felt about each
other?'

'Why? Because it is impossible to do such a thing.
Madre de Dios, Laura! Do you really imagine that
I could ever forgive or forget what you did?' He
caught her suddenly, his hands clasping her
shoulders as he hauled her towards him and glared
down into her face. 'Do you?'

Pain was a sharp edge like glass cutting across
every nerve so that she flinched under its assault,
yet she forced herself to meet his furious gaze. 'If
you loved me, Luis, *really* loved me, then you could
forgive and forget anything!'

'Could I indeed? You think it is that simple?' He
thrust her from him with a suddenness that made
her stagger until she caught hold of the edge of the
desk. When she looked at him she wanted to cry,
wanted to weep for the agony she saw etched on
his face before the mask of composure slid back
into place. He ran a hand over his hair, smoothing

a few black strands back before he glanced at her again.

'You will find everything you need in the middle drawer—paper, envelopes, stamps. I must go now or I shall be late for a meeting. I only dropped by to collect some papers I had forgotten.' He picked up a folder from the edge of the desk. 'If you are still feeling unwell this afternoon, I suggest that you call the doctor.'

He walked towards the door and Laura watched him go, every sweet dream she'd ever harboured dying at her feet. This was the last time she would ever see him, the last time she would ever hear his voice and she didn't know how she was going to bear it. What she had said just now was true, so true that it hurt: if he had loved her then he could have put the past behind him and looked towards the future they would build together. *She* could have done it. Even knowing exactly what he had been planning all these weeks and just how deeply his desire for revenge ran, she could have forgiven him everything if he had met her halfway because she loved him so much. But it wasn't to be.

'Goodbye, Luis.' Her voice was husky with emotion, so quiet that she thought he hadn't heard until he suddenly turned to glance back. Light was spilling through the window, catching him in its slanting golden rays so that for a moment he stood there spotlighted. Laura stared at him hungrily, absorbing the sight of him, letting the image seep deep inside her so that she would remember it for ever. Then without a word he was gone.

She steadied herself against the desk with both hands as her legs started to buckle under the force of the total desolation she felt. She couldn't break down now. She had to be strong... strong enough to leave Luis for good. She had the money her father had left to her in his will—not a fortune but enough to tide her over until the baby was born. She'd been saving it against a rainy day and now that day had arrived. Once she was back on her feet then she could think about finding herself a job, using her teaching credentials to do supply work if there was nothing permanent available. She had a lot more going for her than many women in her situation, with an unworkable marriage behind them. She would survive, but that was all it would be, mere survival, because she would no longer have Luis in her life.

CHAPTER TEN

IT WAS adrenalin that kept her going on the long walk back into town. She didn't dare ask José to drive her or call a taxi, which would only invite speculation. There was no way of knowing how long Luis would be gone and she didn't want any of the servants alerting him as to what was happening as soon as he got back. It was the same need for caution which made her reconsider her first plan to head straight for the airport. The airport would be the first place Luis would check once he realised she had gone.

She found a taxi in town and asked the driver to take her to Cadiz. From there trains ran fairly frequently to Seville where she could catch a plane back to England. It would make it that much more difficult for Luis to track her down.

Hysteria rose in a sudden shocking swirl and she bit her lip as she stared out of the taxi window. She was acting like some sort of master criminal, covering her tracks and taking evasive action. It would have been laughable if it hadn't been so deadly serious. Luis would never forgive her for running away again like this and she wasn't fool enough to think he would.

Just for a moment thoughts of Rachel and what Luis might do to her friend surfaced through the panic, but ruthlessly she blanked them out. She would worry about that later once she was safely out of the country. Luis wasn't omnipotent; there had to be something that she could do to stop him carrying out his threats, although she had even less idea now what it might be than she'd had weeks ago. But, for now, she had to think first and foremost about the baby.

It was late afternoon by the time the taxi dropped her off outside the station. Laura paid the fare without question. All she wanted to do was get on the train and set off on her journey, but when she enquired as to the time of the next train to Seville she was informed that there wouldn't be another one until that evening.

She bought a ticket then wandered back to the street, wondering how to fill in the next few hours. There was a small café tucked down a side street not too far away from the station and she went and sat down at one of the tables outside, ordering coffee when the waiter appeared. She hadn't eaten anything apart from those few bites of toast but she didn't feel hungry.

She sipped the coffee then ordered another, loath to get up and start walking again. The evening rush hour had started and cars milled up and down the streets, engines revving noisily although they barely moved a few feet at a time. Once she thought she heard someone calling her name but when she looked up she couldn't recognise any of the vehicles. She must have been mistaken because she knew no one in Cadiz and no one knew her. It was a strangely empty feeling.

Refusing the waiter's offer of a third cup of coffee, she paid her bill then made her way back, praying that the train would be on time. She didn't need any more delays, more time to sit around and brood about what had happened. She *had* to leave no matter how it hurt to do so. Luis didn't love her.

Tears clouded her vision and she felt in her pocket for a tissue to wipe them away, not noticing the small boy who hurled himself suddenly in front of her. Laura stumbled over him, just managing to right herself before she fell, but the child wasn't so lucky. He fell down with a loud thump and let out a piercing cry more of shock than pain. Laura dropped to her knees, murmuring a few words of comfort in slow Spanish but he was inconsolable. He dragged himself up off the ground and ran across the platform to hurl himself into his father's outstretched arms and bury his face in his shoulder. The man gave Laura an apologetic smile then turned his attention fully to his son, holding him close as he stroked his hair and spoke lovingly to him.

Laura straightened, watching the scene with an ache in her heart. Her child would never be able to turn to his father for comfort; he would never know what it was like to be held close like that little boy, safe in such strong, loving arms. She wanted to do the best she could for this child she was carrying, but was taking him away from Luis and his heritage really the best thing she could do?

The uncertainties seemed to whirl inside her head until she felt dizzy with the speed of them and she went and sat down on a bench, wishing she knew what to do. Everything had seemed to be cut and dried before, but it didn't seem that simple any longer. She loved Luis and she would love this child they had created together, yet she was about to hurt them both in the cruellest way possible. Was that love? How could two wrongs make anything right?

She closed her eyes and let her mind drift back and forth, unaware of the time passing or the people who walked past the bench and paused uncertainly at the sight of the girl who looked so lost and forlorn. It was only when she suddenly became aware of someone standing before her blocking the light cast by the lamp that she opened her eyes and stared up at the tall figure who was watching her.

'Are you all right?'

There was no anger in his voice and that more than anything shocked her out of the trance she seemed to have slipped in to. She sat up straighter, pushing the silky fall of pale hair back from her face as she searched his eyes for the fury he must surely be feeling at what she had done, but there was nothing there but a raw, painful anguish which tore at her heart.

She looked away, not proof against such naked emotion, as she nodded and heard him mutter something under his breath that sounded less like a curse than a harsh utterance of thanks. He dropped down beside her on the bench and dragged his hands through his windswept hair then let them fall to his knees and Laura was shocked to see how they trembled. She looked up at him then, straight into his eyes, and felt something warm start to flow through the coldness which had filled her for so long.

He stared at her as though he was hungry for just the sight of her, his eyes tracing every delicate line of her face. 'I thought I had missed you, that I would not be able to...to find you!'

His voice grated harshly, the smooth tones roughened by an emotion that shocked her into speech. She had never heard Luis sound like this before, as though something was tearing him apart!

'Would it have mattered to you if you hadn't found me, Luis? Really mattered, I mean? Or is it more a question of you hating the idea of me escaping from your clutches and thwarting all your plans?' It was impossible to hide the bitterness she felt. It echoed in her quiet voice and she saw him flinch as though he'd been struck a physical blow. Just for a second he stared at her, then with a speed that left her gasping had her in his arms.

'*Sí*! Yes, it would have mattered, Laura! I wish to God that it didn't, wish that all I wanted from you was revenge, but that isn't so. I have lied to you and to myself for so long, yet now I find that I cannot lie any longer!'

His mouth was rough as it took hers in a kiss that held a raw need. There was none of the skill and finesse that Luis usually employed but Laura didn't object. How could she, when his actions far more than his words told her that everything he'd said was right. She kissed him back with all the pent-up love she'd kept hidden for so long now and felt him shudder deeply.

He drew back slowly, as though reluctant to end the passionate assault on her senses, his eyes glittering as he stared down into her face. 'I love you, *querida*. I did not want to tell you that. I have fought against doing so every day you have been here but now I can fight no longer. I love you.'

She wanted to believe him so much but she'd been hurt too many times before. It made her afraid to let hope blossom. He seemed to sense how she felt because he stood up abruptly pushing his hands into the pockets of his trousers as he stared bleakly down at her. 'It is the truth, *pequeña*. Finally. But I can understand your reluctance to believe it. I knew just as soon as I discovered that you had left me again how I felt.' He laughed bitterly, scant amusement in the sound. 'I have treated you abominably. I have no excuse for my behaviour. I can only apologise and ask that you forgive me. If you wish to leave then I shall not try to stop you.'

'Does...does that mean that you won't carry out all those threats you made, against Rachel and her brother?'

'Yes. You can rest assured of that. You have my word, Laura. All I ask is that before you go we talk to one another about everything that has happened.'

'Talk?' She laughed with a touch of hysteria. 'You want us to talk! About what, Luis? The one thing we ever needed to talk about is the one thing you have continually refused to discuss!'

'I know. Do you think I don't realise that? But now I am giving you the chance you have asked for repeatedly.'

His arrogance took her breath away. 'You are giving me the chance? How very admirable of you!' She stood up abruptly, fighting against tears which stemmed as much from anger as anything else. 'I said all there was to be said this morning. I had to force you to stand and listen, remember? And at the end of it, what did you do? Told me that it made not a scrap of difference to you!'

'I was wrong!' He stood up too, anger tightening his jaw, making his eyes glitter. 'What do you want from me, Laura? Do you want me to beg?'

Suddenly the fight drained out of her and she gave a shaky sigh. 'No. That isn't what I want, Luis.'

His anger seemed to fade also, his face softening as he reached out and touched her cheek with a gentle finger. 'I would do so, *mi esposa*. I would get down here and now on my knees and beg you to listen if it was the only way.'

His tenderness was her undoing. The tears brimmed over and she lowered her head, hearing his rough exclamation, but when he tried to take her into his arms she pushed him away. 'No. Please don't, Luis. That won't solve anything, will it?' She wiped a hand across her eyes then blinked back the rest of the tears. 'What we feel for one another physically could only cloud the issue right now.'

'Would it? I love you, Laura, and I think...hope...that you love me.' His hand cupped her cheek, warm against the cold damp skin. 'The fact that we are so compatible physically is merely a reflection of that love.'

He drew her slowly to him, his arms enfolding her as he looked down into her face. 'Can you really separate the two? Can you put your hand on your heart and say that the magic you feel in my arms is divorced from the love you have for me? If you didn't love me, *amada*, then we would not *make* love so successfully.'

Colour ran hotly into her face and she turned her head so that he couldn't read the answer in her eyes. He laughed then gently put her from him. 'So will you come with me while we talk this through and see if we can find a solution at last?' He glanced impatiently at the milling crowds. 'This is not the place for such a discussion.'

He held his hand out and after a moment's hesitation Laura slid hers into it. Perhaps she was being foolishly premature in hoping that they could work through all the misunderstandings, but she loved him so much it was worth one last try.

They made the journey in silence. There was so much to say yet somehow Laura couldn't find the words now that she needed them. Once they were in the house then it would be different. Then they would have all the time in the world to discuss what had happened. Yet when Luis stopped the car in the driveway she felt a sudden fear run down her spine.

'You were so quiet I thought you were asleep,' he said softly.

'No,' she whispered just as quietly. 'How could I sleep?'

He caught her nervous hands and raised them to his lips and kissed them, smiling when he felt her shiver in reaction. 'It would have done you the world of good, Laura. We have a long night ahead of us.'

She drew her hands away, going cold at the thought. What if Luis still couldn't come to terms with her past after their talk? She didn't think she could bear to have her hopes raised only to have them dashed again. 'It is going to be difficult, Luis, but...'

He stopped her with a gentle finger on her mouth, his eyes dancing with amusement. 'I do not mean this talk we intend to have but what will surely follow later.' His eyes skimmed her body in a look which brought the blood surging along her veins and made her heart thunder wildly.

In a sensual haze she let Luis help her from the car and lead her inside, shivering at the coolness of the interior after the warmth of the night air. It was quite late and everywhere was quiet, the servants retired to their own quarters. When footsteps echoed along the hall, Laura glanced round, wondering if Doña Elena had returned from her trip, then felt herself go cold with shock when she recognised Mercedes.

Horrified, she shot a look at Luis, scarcely able to believe that he had brought her back to talk about their life together knowing that the other woman was in the house.

'Ahhh, I see that Luis found you then, Laura. You do seem to have a penchant for causing him a great deal of trouble.'

Mercedes' words seemed to bring to life every one of her old fears, reminding her so vividly of what they'd spoken of earlier in the day. Had she been a fool to trust Luis so readily? He claimed that he loved her but had it been just a trick to get her back where he wanted her?

With a cry of distress she ran up the stairs and into the bedroom, ignoring Luis's order to stop. She locked the door then leant weakly against it while the tears rolled down her cheeks. How could she have been so naive after everything that had happened? If Luis felt even a fraction of what he professed to then he would never have allowed that woman to be in the house now!

'Laura, open this door! Do you hear me? Open it at once!'

She leapt away from the door as Luis hammered on it, her whole body shaking. 'Go away. I don't ever want to talk to you again!'

'A few minutes ago you were as eager as I to sort things out. Stop playing games!'

'Games? I am not the one playing them, Luis! You are! But I won't let you do this to me...I won't let you trick me again!'

His voice dropped an octave, deliberately soothing although she could hear the impatience under the deep tones. 'You are getting hysterical, Laura. Please open this door so that we can talk.'

'Perhaps I am getting hysterical and who can blame me? Which woman wouldn't get hysterical when she's been tricked into this sort of a situation.'

'I do not understand any of this.' His hand must have struck the door a heavy blow because it shuddered violently under the force of it. '*Dios*, Laura, you owe me an explanation.'

'I don't owe you anything, Luis! But if you are still confused then I suggest you go back downstairs and ask Mercedes about our little chat this afternoon.' She laughed a trifle shrilly, the hysteria he'd mentioned bubbling near to the surface now. 'I'm just surprised that you didn't have her primed to stay away until you had me safely back here in your clutches. Oh, you were almost there, Luis; you almost had me convinced that you meant what you said about loving me and wanting to work this out between us.'

Her voice broke on the last words and she sat down heavily on the bed, too distressed now to even cry. What a fool she had been, a blind, trusting fool yet again!

She had no idea how long she sat there in silence. Time seemed to drift past until the sudden roar of an engine as a car tore away down the drive brought her to her feet. She walked to the window, rubbing her arms to ward off the chill as she watched it travel down the drive. It was Luis's car, she had no difficulty recognising it even at this distance, yet she wasn't surprised. He must be taking Mercedes home, safe in the knowledge that Laura was once more back where he wanted her to be. How he must be laughing to himself at her easy capitulation. A few kisses, a few fervent avowals of love and she'd done exactly what he'd wanted without a fuss, without any unpleasant scene.

She turned away as the tail-lights of the car disappeared, feeling strangely numb, as though all this was happening to someone else and she was just an onlooker watching it unfold. Later she would have to rally herself and decide what to do but for now it seemed to be more effort than she could cope with.

With a sigh she unlocked the door and walked slowly down the stairs towards the kitchen. She'd eaten nothing all day, which could account for this feeling of lightheadedness which assailed her. She had to think about the baby now; that was the most important thing in her life.

Her shoes made a light clicking sound on the marble floor, echoing around the silence, and unconsciously she tried to quieten the sound although there was no one around to hear it. Luis would be at Mercedes' house by now; would he stay the night there with her, free to enjoy her company now that there was no need to pretend about their relationship?

A whimper of pain escaped Laura's lips at the thought and she stopped, clinging hold of the banister rail then jumped with shock when Luis spoke from just behind her.

'Are you all right, Laura?' He reached out to her but she backed away at once, her eyes huge and haunted.

'No. Don't touch me. I . . . I thought you'd gone out . . . taken Mercedes home in your car.'

He shook his head, his dark hair catching the light from the chandelier, his eyes unfathomable as he studied her for a moment then glanced down at the glass he held in one hand. He swirled the whisky round a couple of times then drank it all in one go before setting the glass down on a nearby table with a restrained violence to the action that made her heart leap. 'Mercedes has gone . . . yes. She has driven herself home in my car, seeing as she did not come on her own tonight but had Domingo bring her.'

'I see. Well, I really don't know why you didn't go with her.' She paused, a bitter little smile curling her mouth as she glanced up at where he was still standing. 'But perhaps I do. Were you afraid I would run away again if you didn't watch over me?' She shook her head, feeling her hair brushing heavily against her neck. 'Don't worry, Luis. I'm far too tired to go through all that again tonight.

You shouldn't have denied yourself that way. There was no need now that everything is out in the open.'

His jaw tautened at her cold sarcasm but his voice was level, almost gentle. 'Yes, I stayed to watch over you, Laura, but not to stop you from running away. I stayed in case you needed me, because I was worried about you.' He paused until she lifted her gaze to his, drawn by something she couldn't understand. 'I stayed because I wanted to be with you, *amada*, not Mercedes.'

How she wanted to believe that soft tone, those sweet words but she would never believe him again! 'How touching! Now if you'll excuse me . . .' She went to move past him but he stepped in her path.

'Mercedes told me what had gone on this afternoon, Laura. Oh, she didn't want to, but in the end she did when I insisted.' There was a note in his voice that made a shiver race down Laura's spine and she glanced up at him in alarm, seeing the fury glittering in the very depths of his eyes. Yet surprisingly she knew it wasn't directed at her. She swallowed hard, easing the sudden knot of tension that closed her throat but it was impossible to speak, and Luis carried on.

'I don't think I've heard the whole story—I don't think I want to. My family and Mercedes' has been close for many years, and to even begin to understand the sort of lies she has told you is more than I can handle right now. I just want you to know that Mercedes has gone and that she will never be welcome in this house again.'

It was impossible not to want to believe him, impossible to hear the anger in his voice, see the contempt on his face and still doubt, but she did

because she'd had so many occasions to doubt
before. 'Are you saying that...that...?' She
couldn't seem to go on, her heart in her eyes, her
whole body shaking. Luis swore softly, colourfully,
and took a step closer to her yet didn't touch her.
Laura had the feeling that he was holding himself
in check, afraid of scaring her in any way into
running again, but she had never felt less like
running in her life! It might be madness, folly born
out of desperation, but she believed him!

'That every word she has ever told you was a lie.'
His hand brushed hers in a touch so light yet it
made her tremble, and she felt the tremor race from
her into him. He drew in a sharp breath, his face
all angles, his mouth a thin line of restraint.
'Mercedes and I were never lovers. I give you my
word on that, Laura. I never wanted her or any
other woman from the first moment I met you. I
told myself I should hate you for the way you had
tricked me but it was so hard to do. It was only
pride that made me act the way I did and I am
ashamed of it. I love you—*you*! It makes no difference what happened in your past any longer. I
think I understand now how afraid you were to tell
me, because I too have been afraid today. Afraid
that I had lost you for good.'

'I was. So afraid that you wouldn't want me, but
I never meant to hurt you, Luis! I never intended
to deceive you.'

'I know.' He drew her into his arms, holding her
so gently that she felt tears well into her eyes at his
tenderness. He kissed them away, cupping her chin
in his hand as his lips moved over each damp eyelid.

'I adore you, *mi esposa*. I was yours and only yours, body and soul from the first moment I saw you.'

She laughed shakily, snuggling closer into his hold. 'And I belonged to you too from that moment.' She drew back a fraction, a frown puckering her brow for an instant. 'There was never anything between Domingo and I. I want you to understand that.'

'I know.' He sighed roughly, feathering a delicate kiss across the frown lines to smooth them out. 'I knew it even before he said as much this evening on the telephone.'

'You telephoned him? But I thought you said that you would never . . . never . . .'

'Crawl to him to hear that you had kept your vows? I remember clearly what I said to you, Laura. Every harsh word. Each is engraved on my heart.' He ran a hand down her cheek, his fingers trembling until she turned and pressed her mouth against them.

'Don't, Luis, we both said things we regret.'

'And I shall regret them until the day I die.' His voice throbbed with emotion, his hand curving around her cheek. 'Every cruel word filled my head when I came back and found that you had gone. I think I went slightly crazy, discovering that it had happened again, yet I couldn't blame you for what you had done. It took me a while to think what to do and that was when I phoned Domingo.' He laughed bitterly. 'I even hoped that you were with him just so that I might have the chance to talk to you, maybe convince you not to leave me again.'

'Oh, Luis!' She slid her arms around his waist, holding him close, feeling his pain as though it was

her own. They had hurt each other so much, but
if they could only set that aside then it would make
them stronger.

He smoothed a hand over her hair then kissed
her temple, his lips gentle. 'I owe Domingo a debt.
He not only went out of his way to confirm what
I knew already in my heart, that there was nothing
between you two, but told me that he had seen you
that afternoon in Cadiz. Without that I wouldn't
have known where to start looking for you, Laura.
I would have tried all the likely places but I would
never have found you in time. You would have left.'

She sighed gently, remembering that frantic,
painful flight. 'I didn't want you to. I took care to
cover my tracks, Luis, so that you wouldn't find
me. I knew that the airport here would be the first
place you would look, but Cadiz…I meant to catch
the train to Seville and fly back to England from
there but…' She stopped, colour tinging her cheeks
as she remembered her thoughts, her sudden uncertainties about whether she was doing the right
thing by running and denying Luis any knowledge
of his child.

'But?' he prompted. He studied her face, the fear
he could see still lying in the depths of her shadowed eyes. 'Even now you still aren't sure I am
telling you the truth, are you, Laura? I don't blame
you but I don't know any way to convince
you…apart from this.' His lips settled on hers in
a kiss of such tenderness and love that her heart
seemed to swell with emotion. He wasn't demanding he was giving, giving himself to her, heart
and soul, trusting her with all those secret parts of
him that made him vulnerable. He had never

opened himself to her like this before, never laid his emotions bare, and it touched her more than she could say. To feel Luis, always so strong and indomitable before, now so vulnerable made all the fears fade and trust grow.

'I love you, Laura,' he whispered shakily. 'I have always loved you. I just convinced myself that what I felt was a desire for revenge but it was all lies . . . lies!'

'And I love you too, Luis. Only you . . . and . . . and the child I am carrying.' She took his hand and laid it against her stomach, smiling at the shock which flickered in his eyes.

'You are pregnant? Is that what you are saying, *amada*?'

'Mmmm. I hope you don't mind but I'm afraid you only have yourself to blame for my condition,' she teased gently, loving the expression of awe on his handsome face.

He kissed her hard and hungrily, his mouth fervent with need. 'Mind? It is something I have dreamed about, you carrying my child!'

'Is that the reason why you wanted me to come back to you in the first place, Luis? Because you wanted a child to carry on the name of Rivera?' There was an echo of pain in her soft voice, a faint shadow on her face as she asked the question. She looked down, not wanting to see the truth of it and heard him mutter something rough. He lifted her face, his eyes very dark as they met hers.

'I wanted you back because I loved you, Laura. I made up any number of reasons to hide that fact from myself but that is the truth. This child we will have is just a beautiful bonus.'

'But Mercedes said...' She stopped when she saw the anger on his face but his voice was gentle.

'She said what? Please tell me, Laura. I don't want there to be any secrets between us.'

'She said that you were desperate for an heir, that...that the only reason you wanted to continue with this mockery of a marriage was because it was the one way you could get a child when it isn't possible for you to divorce me.'

'I never, ever discussed either our marriage or children with her. I want you to believe that, Laura. Never!'

There was no way she could doubt him, not when she saw that certainty on his face. She reached up and kissed him. 'I do. I had only found out for certain that I was pregnant this morning, just before I met Mercedes in town. When she told me that I was so afraid, Luis. She said that once I'd produced a child then you would no longer need me in your life. You would have the child and that would be enough!'

'And that is what pushed you into running away again.' He drew her to him, holding her close as though he would never let her leave his embrace. 'Mercedes is very astute. Perhaps she guessed somehow that you were pregnant from something you said.'

'No. I didn't know myself until last night when I started adding up the clues...' She paused for a moment. 'This morning, though...' She stopped but Luis prompted her.

'What happened then?'

'Just something Pilar said.' She laughed with a touch of embarrassment. 'I had the feeling that

Pilar had guessed even though I hadn't done so myself.'

Luis sighed deeply. 'And that solves the mystery.' At her start of surprise he continued, 'Pilar's sister, Rosa, works for Mercedes. They probably discussed the news of your condition and somehow Mercedes heard and used it to her advantage. I shall never forgive her for what she has tried to do, Laura.'

It made sense, so much sense that Laura wondered why she hadn't realised sooner what the woman was up to. Mercedes had used whatever scraps of information she had gleaned to her advantage time and again. It explained everything apart from where Luis had gone last night. She frowned, wondering if she should ask him, and heard him laugh deeply.

'Tell me what is bothering you now, *querida*. We must clear this all up once and for all, and soon.'

She glanced up at him questioningly. 'Soon?'

'*Sí*. We are wasting time, too much time which could be employed in a much more enjoyable way.' He smoothed his hand down her side, the tips of his fingers brushing against the curve of her breast, and she shuddered. When he did it again with a touch of knowing arrogance she went up on tiptoe and kissed his mouth then just as deliberately gently bit his lower lip. He groaned deeply, his arms contracting around her, his body pulsing against hers in a way that left her in no doubt as to his need.

'You are a witch, Laura. You cast a spell over me all those months ago and I cannot be held responsible for my actions. So tell me quickly what you wish to know!'

She stroked her hand across his chest, feeling the thunderous beat of his heart against her palm. She let it rest there, loving him more than she'd thought possible. 'Where did you go last night, Luis, when you left the house? I thought you'd spent the night with Mercedes, especially after what she said to me today, but now I don't know.'

He captured her hand and kissed the palm, folding her fingers over the warm spot where his lips had caressed. 'I didn't go anywhere. I just drove and drove trying to make some sense out of all the madness that seemed to be filling my head. No matter what Mercedes told you, I never went to her. How could I, when all I could think about was you?'

'And you didn't plan that trip to Amsterdam with her either?'

'No!' He seemed to make a determined effort to control the sudden flash of anger. 'I was surprised to see her there but thought nothing of it, merely assumed that she was there on business. If she told you anything different then it was lies, Laura. I cannot believe that you could be taken in that way!'

'Can't you?' She laughed lightly. 'Then you must never have known what it feels like to be jealous, Luis.'

His face softened at once. 'Oh, but I do. I seem to have been eaten up with jealousy for so long now, but there is no need for me to feel that way any longer.'

'No. There never was a need. It was always you, Luis. Only you. You are the man of my dreams, the man who fills my heart.' She let her head rest against his chest, feeling the deep shuddering breath he drew in. There was a moment's long silence, as though both of them were suddenly aware of how close they had come to losing one another. Then Luis bent and lifted her into his arms, kissing her softly before drawing back to look deep into her eyes. 'Now all that is behind us, Laura. From this point on we look to our future. Tonight you will sleep in my arms and when we awake tomorrow it will be a new beginning for all of us—you, me and the child you will give me in a few months' time. I love you, *querida*.'

She cupped his cheek with a gentle hand, her eyes filled with everything she felt. 'And I love you too, *querido*.' Her hand slid around his neck as he carried her up the stairs, her heart swelling with joy at the thought of the life they would have together. A new beginning with the man she loved with all her heart.

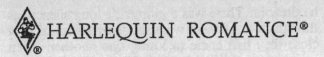

HARLEQUIN ROMANCE®

Coming Next Month

#3379 BRIDES FOR BROTHERS Debbie Macomber
The first book in **Midnight Sons**, a very special new six-book series from this bestselling author.

Welcome to Hard Luck, Alaska. Location: 50 miles north of the Arctic Circle. Population: 150—but it'll be growing soon! Because this town is determined to attract women. The campaign is spearheaded by the O'Halloran brothers, who run a small-plane charter service called Midnight Sons. Thanks to them, things are going to change in Hard Luck—maybe more than anyone expects....

In *Brides for Brothers* meet Sawyer O'Halloran, one of the Midnight Sons, and Abbey Sutherland from Seattle, librarian and divorced mother of two young children. Abbey's first of the women to arrive in Hard Luck—but she hasn't told anyone she's arriving with kids!

#3380 THE BEST MAN Shannon Waverly
Kayla Brayton remembered Matt Reed as a handsome, self-assured twenty-one-year-old, and she fully expected a handsome, self-assured thirty-one-year-old. She wasn't disappointed! Matt was the kind of man every girl dreamed of, but was he the best man for her?

#3381 ONCE BURNED Margaret Way
Family Ties
Guy Harcourt was strong, forceful and dynamic. He was also irresistible to women. And Celine Langston was no exception. She had never wanted anyone as much as him. But she was like a moth caught in a candle's flame, and once burned...

#3382 LEGALLY BINDING Jessica Hart
Sealed with a Kiss
Jane was a sensible girl—everyone said so. Ten years ago she'd been far too sensible to run away with the local rebel, Lyall Harding. But now Lyall was back and the bad boy had grown into a successful businessman. Was now the time to throw caution to the wind?

AVAILABLE THIS MONTH:

#3375 THE BABY CAPER
Emma Goldrick

#3376 ONE-NIGHT WIFE
Day Leclaire

#3377 FOREVER ISN'T LONG ENOUGH
Val Daniels

#3378 ANGELS DO HAVE WINGS
Helen Brooks

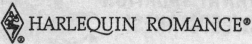

HARLEQUIN ROMANCE®

brings you

Legally Binding by JESSICA HART

Jane Makepeace was a sensible girl—everyone said so. Ten years ago she'd been far too levelheaded to run away with Lyall Harding, the town's die-hard rebel. But now Jane was a sensible woman with a problem.... Lyall Harding was back and the bad boy had made more than good. Worse, he seemed to hold Jane's future in his hands.

The last letter from her bank manager had hardly been sealed with anything like affection. It was a warning of the dire state of her finances. She badly needed to win the contract from Lyall's company to keep her business afloat. Unfortunately, he seemed to have a different idea of negotiation than Jane and was more than prepared to use their old attraction as a bargaining chip. She didn't feel they were making any progress—in work at least. Unless, of course, kisses could be considered legally binding?

Coming next month, from the bestselling author of
A SENSIBLE WIFE. JESSICA HART has recently
been nominated for a *Romantic Times* award.

FLYAWAY VACATION SWEEPSTAKES!

This month's destination:

Exciting ORLANDO, FLORIDA!

Are you the lucky person who will win a free trip to Orlando? Imagine how much fun it would be to visit Walt Disney World**, Universal Studios**, Cape Canaveral and the other sights and attractions in this area! The Next page contains tow Official Entry Coupons, as does each of the other books you received this shipment. Complete and return *all* the entry coupons—**the more times you enter, the better your chances of winning!**

Then keep your fingers crossed, because you'll find out by October 15, 1995 if you're the winner! If you are, here's what you'll get:

- Round-trip airfare for two to Orlando!
- 4 days/3 nights at a first-class resort hotel!
- $500.00 pocket money for meals and sightseeing!

Remember: The more times you enter, the better your chances of winning!*

*NO PURCHASE OR OBLIGATION TO CONTINUE BEING A SUBSCRIBER NECESSARY TO ENTER. SEE BACK PAGE FOR ALTERNATIVE MEANS OF ENTRY AND RULES.

**THE PROPRIETORS OF THE TRADEMARKS ARE NOT ASSOCIATED WITH THIS PROMOTION.

VOR KAL

FLYAWAY VACATION
SWEEPSTAKES

OFFICIAL ENTRY COUPON

This entry must be received by: SEPTEMBER 30, 1995
This month's winner will be notified by: OCTOBER 15, 1995
Trip must be taken between: NOVEMBER 30, 1995-NOVEMBER 30, 1996

YES, I want to win the vacation for two to Orlando, Florida. I understand the prize includes round-trip airfare, first-class hotel and $500.00 spending money. Please let me know if I'm the winner!

Name_____

Address _____ Apt. _____

City   State/Prov.   Zip/Postal Code

Account #_____

Return entry with invoice in reply envelope.

© 1995 HARLEQUIN ENTERPRISES LTD.   COR KAL

FLYAWAY VACATION
SWEEPSTAKES

OFFICIAL ENTRY COUPON

This entry must be received by: SEPTEMBER 30, 1995
This month's winner will be notified by: OCTOBER 15, 1995
Trip must be taken between: NOVEMBER 30, 1995-NOVEMBER 30, 1996

YES, I want to win the vacation for two to Orlando, Florida. I understand the prize includes round-trip airfare, first-class hotel and $500.00 spending money. Please let me know if I'm the winner!

Name_____

Address _____ Apt. _____

City   State/Prov.   Zip/Postal Code

Account #_____

Return entry with invoice in reply envelope.

© 1995 HARLEQUIN ENTERPRISES LTD.   COR KAL

OFFICIAL RULES

FLYAWAY VACATION SWEEPSTAKES 3449

NO PURCHASE OR OBLIGATION NECESSARY

Three Harlequin Reader Service 1995 shipments will contain respectively, coupons for entry into three different prize drawings, one for a trip for two to San Francisco, another for a trip for two to Las Vegas and the third for a trip for two to Orlando, Florida. To enter any drawing using an Entry Coupon, simply complete and mail according to directions.

There is no obligation to continue using the Reader Service to enter and be eligible for any prize drawing. You may also enter any drawing by hand printing the words "Flyaway Vacation," your name and address on a 3"x5" card and the destination of the prize you wish that entry to be considered for (i.e., San Francisco trip, Las Vegas trip or Orlando trip). Send your 3"x5" entries via first-class mail (limit: one entry per envelope) to: Flyaway Vacation Sweepstakes 3449, c/o Prize Destination you wish that entry to be considered for, P.O. Box 1315, Buffalo, NY 14269-1315, USA or P.O. Box 610, Fort Erie, Ontario L2A 5X3, Canada.

To be eligible for the San Francisco trip, entries must be received by 5/30/95; for the Las Vegas trip, 7/30/95; and for the Orlando trip, 9/30/95.

Winners will be determined in random drawings conducted under the supervision of D.L. Blair, Inc., an independent judging organization whose decisions are final, from among all eligible entries received for that drawing. San Francisco trip prize includes round-trip airfare for two, 4-day/3-night weekend accommodations at a first-class hotel, and $500 in cash (trip must be taken between 7/30/95—7/30/96, approximate prize value—$3,500); Las Vegas trip prize includes round-trip airfare for two, 4-day/3-night weekend accommodations at a first-class hotel, and $500 in cash (trip must be taken between 9/30/95—9/30/96, approximate prize value—$3,500); Orlando trip includes round-trip airfare for two, 4-day/3-night weekend accommodations at a first-class hotel, and $500 in cash (trip must be taken between 11/30/95—11/30/96, approximate prize value—$3,500). All travelers must sign and return a Release of Liability prior to travel. Hotel accommodations and flights are subject to accommodation and schedule availability. Sweepstakes open to residents of the U.S. (except Puerto Rico) and Canada, 18 years of age or older. Employees and immediate family members of Harlequin Enterprises, Ltd., D.L. Blair, Inc., their affiliates, subsidiaries and all other agencies, entities and persons connected with the use, marketing or conduct of this sweepstakes are not eligible. Odds of winning a prize are dependent upon the number of eligible entries received for that drawing. Prize drawing and winner notification for each drawing will occur no later than 15 days after deadline for entry eligibility for that drawing. Limit: one prize to an individual, family or organization. All applicable laws and regulations apply. Sweepstakes offer void wherever prohibited by law. Any litigation within the province of Quebec respecting the conduct and awarding of the prizes in this sweepstakes must be submitted to the Regies des loteries et Courses du Quebec. In order to win a prize, residents of Canada will be required to correctly answer a time-limited arithmetical skill-testing question. Value of prizes are in U.S. currency.

Winners will be obligated to sign and return an Affidavit of Eligibility within 30 days of notification. In the event of noncompliance within this time period, prize may not be awarded. If any prize or prize notification is returned as undeliverable, that prize will not be awarded. By acceptance of a prize, winner consents to use of his/her name, photograph or other likeness for purposes of advertising, trade and promotion on behalf of Harlequin Enterprises, Ltd., without further compensation, unless prohibited by law.

For the names of prizewinners (available after 12/31/95), send a self-addressed, stamped envelope to: Flyaway Vacation Sweepstakes 3449 Winners, P.O. Box 4200, Blair, NE 68009.

RVC KAL